BOOK OF THE DEAD

A TALE OF TERROR FOR THE 21ˢᵗ CENTURY

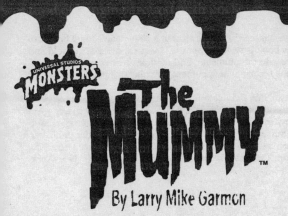

UNIVERSAL STUDIOS MONSTERS

The MUMMY™

By Larry Mike Garmon

SCHOLASTIC INC.

New York   Toronto   London   Auckland   Sydney
Mexico City   New Delhi   Hong Kong   Buenos Aires

No part of this publication may be reproduced in whole or in part, or stored in a retrieval system, or transmitted in any form or by any means, electronic, mechanical, photocopying, recording, or otherwise, without written permission of the publisher. For information regarding permission, write to Scholastic Inc., Attention: Permissions Department, 555 Broadway, New York, NY 10012.

ISBN 0-439-30346-X

Designed by Peter Koblish

12 11 10 9 8 7 6 5 4 3 2   2 3 4 5 6 7/0
Printed in the U.S.A.
First Scholastic printing, February 2002

For my mummy, Patricia Sanders,
whose love of reading
opened up worlds to me

PROLOGUE
Wednesday, 11:13 P.M.
San Tomas Inlet Convention Center

"Do you need anything else before I leave, Professor?" Karl Homer asked as he put down the cup of steaming tea.

Homer stepped back from the big, highly polished oak desk and looked at the professor. To the casual observer, it would appear that Professor Tovar was ignoring his assistant. The professor was mumbling to himself as he scanned a tattered, ancient piece of parchment through a magnifying glass.

Karl Homer, however, knew that the professor wasn't ignoring him, nor was he just mumbling. Professor Angus Tovar was lost deep in concentration, trying to decipher a parchment of papyrus that had arrived earlier that afternoon. The text of Egyptian hieroglyphics had been a peculiar puzzle even for a man renowned as the authority on ancient Egyptian texts, and Professor Tovar had been hovering over the parchment and mumbling for the better part of five hours.

"Professor," Homer said softly as he tapped on the oak desk.

"Huh?" Tovar said, jerking his head up. The thick lenses of his glasses made his eyes appear twice their normal size. He had the look of a man who had been up for days without sleep — gray stubble, haggard eyes, wrinkled seersucker suit. His long, pepper-gray hair stood out in all directions. "Oh, sorry, Karl. I didn't hear you come in."

Homer smiled. "Have you deciphered the papyrus yet?"

"Yes," the professor replied, a smile crossing his face. He put the magnifying glass down and brought the cup of tea to his lips. "Just a few minutes ago," he added. "I was just going over it once more. It's actually amazing. Hieroglyphics were usually only used for such things as royal edicts or inscriptions on the tombs of the pharaohs. Upper-class Egyptians used a form of writing called hieratic, while common Egyptians used a form of writing called demotic."

"Yes, I know," Homer said, seating himself on a leather chair just opposite the desk.

Professor Tovar looked over the edge of his teacup at his assistant. "Ah, yes. Of course you do." He put the cup down and picked the papyrus up by its edges. He chuckled. "This, however, has been a bit of a puzzle. My colleagues at the university couldn't understand it because they were looking for something other than what this really is." He scanned the ancient text once more, then laid it down. "It seems this is nothing more than a scribe's practical joke."

"What do you mean?" Homer said, leaning closer to get a better look at the text.

Professor Tovar used a small, pointed wooden stick to trace each image of the hieroglyphic message. "Texts written in hieroglyphics were usually in praise of a pharaoh or his queen or any of the myriad of gods in the Egyptian pantheon. This" — he tapped the edge of the text gently with the stick — "is nothing more than the Egyptian equivalent of a joke."

Homer stood and moved around to the side of the desk to get a better look at the text. His eyes followed the images of hawks and heads of men and feathers and rivers and rabbits and a dozen other pictographs. A small smile creased his weatherworn leathery face. "I can see how the others at the university missed this."

The professor laughed and clapped Homer on the back. "I knew you'd get it right away once you knew what you were looking for. Those hacks back at the university kept ignoring what was right in front of their eyes. They insisted this was a lost segment of the Papyrus of Ani when actually it's nothing more than a neophyte scribe telling some boyhood joke."

Homer moved back to the front of the desk. "It's late and I really must be leaving. Do you need anything else?"

"Huh?" the professor said, without looking up from the papyrus. "Oh, no, no. You can go home, my old friend. Just make sure to lock up. I've got some work to do before the opening on Monday. We've got the volunteers coming on Saturday for orientation, and I want to make sure that everything is in its proper place."

"I still don't like the idea of using teenagers to help with the exhibits, Professor," Homer said with a frown.

"Nonsense," Tovar replied. "One purpose of the exhibits is to interest young people in the science of archaeology. Our numbers have been dwindling for years. No one seems interested in the past anymore. Pretty soon, archaeologists will be as dead as the scribe who wrote this joke." He lifted up the edge of the papyrus and the corner crumbled. "Dust in the wind." The professor picked up a yellow slip of paper and read from it. "A Mrs. Hoving at the high school is our coordinator. She'll be around on Friday with a list of the students and their assignments."

"I'll lock up," Homer said. "And I'll put a wake-up call into the motel's front desk for six-thirty A.M. Okay?"

"Thank you, Karl," Tovar said. "Get a good night's rest. We're going to be busy for the next few days. I'm going to wait until the security guard comes on at midnight."

"Good night," Homer said. He turned and walked out of the room.

"Good man," the professor mumbled under his breath. He sighed, pushed his glasses up onto the top of his head, and rubbed his eyes. He had been sitting at the desk for hours, mulling over the final details for the grand opening and then amusing himself with the papyrus that had arrived that afternoon. He chuckled silently, picked up the papyrus gently, and shook his head. The problem with his colleagues was that they took themselves too seriously, he reflected. They always wanted to discover that one missing piece, that one long-lost scroll that would write their names in the annals of archaeological history. Sometimes, the professor mused, the experts couldn't see the papyrus for the sheaves.

He set the papyrus down and lifted the teacup to his lips when deep thunder resonated throughout the building, making the windows rattle. The professor started and inadvertently spilled a few droplets of tea on his desk.

"Goodness gracious!" He set the teacup down and quickly began sopping up the spill.

What a child I am! he said to himself. *To be frightened by thunder!*

He had been in San Tomas Inlet for little over a week and since that time had been witness to some of the most terrific and terrifying thunder and lightning storms he had ever seen. Local residents had told him that the storms were on the wane and San Tomas would soon be in the twilight season between winter and spring.

Professor Tovar was amused at the local San Tomas Inlet residents. In the few days he had been in town to set up the exhibition, he had heard rumors that San Tomas was cursed. Vampires, werewolves, the dead coming back to life. He chuckled. It was the same no matter where in the world he traveled. The locals always seemed to have some sort of superstition about the dead or about evil spirits that tormented the living. He knew that all myths were based on a little truth, and he also knew that the "little truth" was often greatly eclipsed by the shadows of superstition.

Professor Tovar chuckled. He definitely had to assign some of his graduate students to conduct a field study of the San Tomas Inlet citizens and their affinity for monster stories.

The windows and the walls shook with a deep moaning sound once more.

Moaning? Nonsense, the professor told himself. *All this talk of monsters has got me imagining things.*

Professor Tovar walked out of his office and locked the door. What he needed was a good night's rest. The teenagers would be coming on Saturday, and he had better be well rested if he intended to keep up with them.

He was nearly to the community center's double front doors when he heard another moan. Only this time, it wasn't a moan. It was more like the sound of two large, heavy stones being rubbed against each other, as one might hear when removing the lid from a stone sarcophagus. Professor Tovar recognized that noise instantly from his years of archaeological study. It made the hair on the back of his neck stand straight up.

The professor turned and peered down the dark hallway. Although he had been there only a week, the professor knew the convention center by heart. For forty years he had crawled around in the dark, claustrophobic tombs of ancient pharaohs and caverns where primitive humans had made their homes, and this experience had taught him to quickly learn the ins and outs of any buildings he spent time in.

What danger could there be here? he asked

himself. He shook his head. Perhaps he was getting too old for this kind of work. Maybe forty years of studying humankind's greatest fears had finally planted a seed of fear within his own logical and studious brain. *Nonsense!* he told himself. *I'm not afraid of anything — I'm a scientist.*

He started off down the hallway, the pant legs of his seersucker suit swishing.

The San Tomas Inlet Convention Center was one of the largest buildings in the small resort town. The building was used primarily as a community center. Most of the conventions that came to Florida opted for the more resplendent offerings of Miami or Palm Beach. San Tomas Inlet had little to offer other than good beaches and a small-town atmosphere.

Professor Tovar made his way down the entry hallway and turned right. The convention center was built in a round maze of rooms and corridors leading to a center theater. Aided only by the security light in each room, Professor Tovar made his way through the various eras of Western civilization. Finally he reached his favorite room, the Egyptian room, where he displayed the treasures of an ancient queen he had discovered during one of his digs in the Valley of the Kings.

It was to this room, the room of the Sleeping

Queen, that Professor Tovar had devoted most of his energy and time, and so, when he flipped on the light, he knew instantly that something was awry. The heavy stone lid of the queen's sarcophagus had been moved, revealing the mummy inside. A fury arose in Professor Tovar. No one was to open the sarcophagus without him present.

He walked over to the stone tomb and examined the outer casing of the mummy. It was intact, the tempered gold-leaf mask of the queen gleaming in the room's light. A scarab amulet still rested on the queen's chest. The inlaid gold and jewels on her crown had not been disturbed.

Professor Tovar tried to slide the stone lid back into place, but it was too heavy for him. He walked around the room, taking a mental inventory. The queen's couch, carved and painted like a leopard, sat near her final resting place. A long table painted with the symbols of ancient Egyptian royalty — hawks, monkeys, scarabs, slaves, jackals — sat against the wall, displaying all the things an Egyptian queen would need in her afterlife: a mirror with a makeup kit, a board game of jackals and wolves, a comb made from bone, gold jewelry emblazoned with fine gems, a mummified cat, and the four canopic jars that contained her entrails.

The professor was already angry and now he became even angrier. The lids of the canopic jars had been removed. The clay heads were shaped like a human head, the head of a falcon, the head of a jackal, and the head of a baboon, representing the four sons of the god Horus.

The professor shook his head and frowned. Some dim-witted graduate student had probably taken the lids off to see what was inside. All the student would have found were the dusty remains of what had once been the queen's liver, lungs, intestines, and stomach. Tovar crossed the room, picked up the jar of Imset, the head of a man, and replaced the lid.

The air was suddenly filled with a dry gray dust, and he sneezed. The force of the sneeze almost caused him to knock over the jar. He caught it just as it teetered on the edge of the queen's table. He took out a handkerchief from his back pocket, wiped his brow, and then rubbed his nose. *The dust must have come from the jar,* he thought.

A fly brushed up against Professor Tovar's cheek and he swatted it away. Then something flicked past his ear. He rubbed his ear and turned around.

"What the devil —" he began, but he never got to finish his sentence.

A rough hand had him about the throat. Instinctively, Tovar grabbed his assailant's wrist and tried to wrest his hand away. The glasses he had placed on top of his head fell to his nose, and if he could have screamed, he would have. For now he could clearly see that this was no man trying to strangle him. It was the mummified remains of the priest he had found buried with the queen.

The professor stared into the hollow eye sockets of the long-dead priest. The dried and cracked skin was pulled taut against the skull. The lips of the dead priest were black and curled back, and the professor could see that the front teeth had been knocked out and the tongue ripped from its roots.

Dark circles began to swim in front of the professor's eyes. His legs and arms began to flail as his body jerked from the lack of oxygen. His arms knocked off the various items on the queen's table, scattering them across the room. Then his arms hit one of the jars, the jar with the baboon head. The jar tottered and then fell to the floor, smashing into clay shards. A fine gray dust floated in the air.

The mummy suddenly released Tovar, and the professor fell to the floor. His lungs burned as he sucked in large gulps of air and dust. The mummy was kneeling next to the broken jar. Garbled sounds emanated from the tongueless mouth. He reached into the pile of gray dust that once had been the queen's lungs and lifted his hands upward, repeating the garbled chant.

Professor Tovar felt the blood rushing in his ears and his heart pounding through his chest. He rose to his feet as quickly as his legs would allow and wobbled from the room. He stumbled through the maze of time, his old legs giving out from under him again and again.

Darkness began to fall across Professor Tovar's mind. He fought to stay conscious. From somewhere deep in the dark gray folds of his mind he remembered that a security guard was coming on duty. Someone who could help him. Someone who could fight off the mummy that had attacked him.

The entrance to the convention center came into view. He reached for the doors, then realized that they were still a good fifty yards away. He fell to his knees and began to crawl, his heart pounding. Each breath was a labor. He kept reaching and he kept failing. He fell to the tiled floor, exhausted. He slowly turned and looked back down the hallway.

The mummy moved slowly toward him, dragging one leg, the bandages slipping with each lurch of the dead priest. The mummy continued his chant.

Then the professor heard it — the high-pitched squeal of a baboon. A shadow shot out from behind the mummy, its mouth emitting a high-pitched squeal of ancient rage and hate.

That squeal was the last sound Professor Tovar heard. Except for his own scream of terror as the baboon sank its teeth into his throat.

CHAPTER ONE
Friday, 2:00 P.M.
Hallway, Ponce de Leon High School

"Nina. Nina!"

The hallways between classes at Ponce High were crowded, noisy, and not easy to navigate or hold a conversation. The dark-haired girl knew that she probably wouldn't be heard, but she tried again.

"NINA!"

Nina Nobriega jerked her head from behind her locker door and smiled. "Hey, Angela," she said as she grabbed a humanities text from her locker.

"Hey, yourself. Where have you been the last few days?" Angela Chavarria tried to sound angry, but she couldn't help being happy to see her friend.

"Oh, you know, the usual things any red-blooded American girl does: listen to music, talk on the phone, hassle parents, fight monsters."

"And ignore your best friend!" Angela added, pretending to pout.

Nina shut her locker. "Sorry about that." They started down the crowded hallway, shouldering their way through the maze of students. "We really had to work fast on this one."

"Yeah, I heard about Frankenstein."

"How did you find out?"

"Rumors have a tendency to fly around this school."

"Uh-huh." Nina pushed past through a couple about to kiss. "So who told you about old Frankie?"

"Captain Bob sat at my table during lunch."

"Say no more," Nina said, laughing. "I bet he said that he was the big hero again."

"Actually, he didn't do much of the talking. That new kid, Trey, said that Bob was the big hero."

"Bob's got Trey convinced that he's some kind of super monster fighter."

"Don't you think Captain Bob looks kind of cute with his head shaved?"

Nina gagged. "Captain Bob wouldn't look cute if he wore a Ben Affleck suit."

"I think you ought to lighten up on the guy," Angela said.

Nina eyed her friend. *Could Angela be falling*

for a nerdy freshman? No way. At least, I hope not.

"Why didn't you call me to help?" Angela asked. "I've got a little experience fighting monsters."

"That's an understatement!" Nina said, grinning. Five months earlier, school had just started at Ponce de Leon High School, and Nina had been looking forward to her junior year, hoping to keep up her perfect grade-point average and maybe meet a special guy. Her parents wouldn't let her date her freshman and sophomore years, so she was determined to finally shed her nerdy image and find a good-looking guy with a few brains in his head.

But it didn't help that two freshmen — Joe Motley and the aforementioned Captain Bob Hardin — seemed to follow her everywhere, ruining her chances with any date candidates in the junior and senior classes.

Then Angela's boyfriend, Todd Gentry, had been attacked by a giant wolf and nearly killed. Nina had decided to put off her hunt for a boyfriend and help Angela while Todd recovered.

That's when the real trouble began. With the help of Captain Bob and Joe, she had discovered that Todd's attacker had not been a giant wolf — it was the greatest bloodsucker of all time, Count Dracula. The one from the

1931 movie that she and the two freshmen had been watching a month earlier. This time, however, the Dean of the Dead didn't come back as a pasty-faced Transylvanian with a Hungarian accent. Instead, the vampire appeared as the handsome Dr. Abel Dunn, dentist at the San Tomas All-Night Dental Clinic. And this time, the bloodsucker wanted to make her best friend, Angela Chavarria, his queen.

Why did I ever let those two boys talk me into taking that projector? Nina thought, chiding herself.

She had had a fun summer working at Universal Studios Florida, and when Joe and Bob had approached her about helping them "borrow" the experimental three-dimensional projector, her love of classic horror movies was more than her curiosity could stand. So, she relented. Of course, she had lived to regret her decision ever since that night, when the projector had been struck by lightning and the six monsters had been released, flesh and blood, into the world.

At first she didn't believe Captain Bob and his theory that the monsters had been released. Bob was intelligent, but he lacked common sense and wasn't the easiest person to be around at times. He never combed his hair, he told bad jokes, he didn't like smart girls, and he thought that peanut butter and bologna sandwiches were a major part of the food chain. Not until she actually came face-to-face with the fearsome Count Dracula did Nina realize that reality had taken on a whole new meaning for her and that the saying "art imitates life" was no longer just a saying.

A little experience? Nina thought. *Girl, you've had enough experience with real evil to make the Spanish Inquisition look like a bunch of funny fellows.*

"All that with Frankenstein happened so quickly," Nina explained. "We didn't have time to get help. Believe me, we could have used it."

"Yeah, you say that now that all the fun's over."

"Believe me, Angela, it wasn't fun." Nina's voice had lost its lilt and she walked a little more slowly. "None of this has been fun. I'd much rather have spent my junior year chasing guys who aren't worth my time than chasing monsters who are trying to kill my best friends."

They walked in silence for a few moments.

Nina asked "How's Todd doing?" Both Todd and his father had been among Dracula's first victims. But since Nina, Joe, and Bob had used Universal's experimental technology to put Dracula back in his movie, the victims had made a miraculous recovery.

"He's okay. He still has a hard time believing it all. His dad does, too. They both think we're a couple of nuts."

"Maybe we are," Nina said as they reached Mrs. Hoving's classroom. "I wake up in the middle of the night either screaming or laughing. Someday I hope I wake up and find out this has been one long, scary dream."

"I'll meet you in the parking lot after school," Angela said, and she dove into the crowd, heading for her creative writing class.

"How's Vampira doing these days?" Stacy McDonald said as Nina entered her humanities class. Three girls seated around Stacy giggled.

Just what I need: Little Miss Manners and her gaggle, Nina thought. She didn't know how Stacy had gotten wind of Angela's experience with Dracula, and she didn't want to know. So she ignored them and took her seat at the front of the third row.

The bell rang, but the students kept talking. Mrs. Hoving, who had been seated behind her desk looking through some papers, peered over the glasses that sat on the tip of her nose. She cleared her throat, and the students stopped talking. All but Stacy and the three girls seated around her.

"Stacy," Mrs. Hoving said in a gentle but firm voice. "I believe the bell has rung."

"I believe you are correct," Stacy said with a

sarcastic smile. The other girls tried to stifle their snickers.

Mrs. Hoving frowned. "Do you also believe that I control your destiny?"

"Huh?" Stacy said, genuinely confused.

"Do you also believe that I control your destiny?"

Stacy raised an eyebrow. "If you mean do I think you're God, no I don't."

"That's not what I mean at all," Mrs. Hoving said. "However, during the time of two-oh-five to three P.M., Monday through Friday, I am the master of your destiny, and when that bell rings, you get quiet or you get lunch detention."

"But we were only talking," Stacy protested.

Mrs. Hoving raised her hand, palm out, a sign that anything else out of Stacy's mouth would mean a week of sitting at the detention table with the dregs of the school. Stacy grimaced, crossed her arms, and kept her mouth shut.

"Now, I have your assignments for the exhibition. Some of you only have to work a couple of nights, and some of you" — she looked directly at Stacy — "have to work at least five nights to earn the extra credit to pass this class."

"Can we work as many nights as we want even if we don't need the extra credit?" Nina asked. She was very excited about the exhibition and wanted to spend as much time there as she could. Archaeology had always been an interest of Nina's.

"You can work as many nights as you like," Mrs. Hoving said. "Just don't overdo it. You have other classes and things to do."

"Sure she does," Stacy said sarcastically, with just enough volume for Nina to hear.

Here we go again, Nina thought as she sighed. For some reason Stacy McDonald had been trying to pick a fight with her for the past two weeks. Nina hadn't done anything to bring about Stacy's ire, or at least nothing she could remember. She knew that Stacy was still upset about the Camryn Manheim comment, but, hey, that had been thrust in fair play, and it wasn't Nina's fault that Stacy wasn't smart enough to have a quick retort.

"You're all to meet with Professor Tovar at the convention center at eleven A.M. tomorrow morning," Mrs. Hoving said. "Each group will have a graduate assistant who will teach you what to do." Mrs. Hoving looked over the edge of her glasses at the students. She pursed her lips, sighed, and then said, "And please, for heaven's sake, don't break anything. The exhibits you'll be handling are real, some thousands of years old, and irreplaceable. You are dealing with ancient history and I hope that if I've taught you anything in this class, I've taught you to respect the past and learn from it."

"Taught me to be bored is more like it," Stacy muttered with a smirk.

Mrs. Hoving sighed, grabbed a yellow pad, and began scribbling on it.

The class "oohed" as Mrs. Hoving wrote. They all knew what she was doing. Stacy could pencil "detention" into her schedule for the rest of the week.

Stacy sat with her mouth open, wanting to protest but knowing that any other sound would increase the punishment to two weeks.

Obviously, Nina thought, *Stacy hasn't learned the most important lesson of history: not repeating the same mistakes over and over again.*

5:45 P.M.
Beach Burger

"Hey, Hubert, throw on some fries," Bob called over his shoulder. He watched out of the corner of his eye as the lanky teen tossed a scoop of frozen french fries into the basket and lowered them into the scalding brown grease. Bob scribbled on the order pad in front of him and announced, "Your total comes to twelve dollars and fifty-nine cents."

"That hamburger better be ground chuck," the man snarled as he fished in his wallet and pulled out a twenty-dollar bill.

Bob shrugged and smiled. "Did you want that to go?"

The man nodded. Bob took the twenty and gave the customer his change. Then he put his right hand on a large glass pickle jar that sat next to the register. He drummed the lip of the jar with his finger and put on the cheesiest smile he could muster.

"What?" the man said. Then he looked at the jar. Slowly, he read, "'Tipping is not the capital of China.'" The man frowned and sighed. "You want a tip?"

Bob's smile grew larger and more plastic. "Sure," he said through his teeth.

Without smiling, the man said, "Don't use so much polish on that bald head of yours. It's blinding." The man walked away, sat at a booth, and waited for his food, never looking in Bob's direction.

Hubert snorted a laugh, and Bob's smile became a grimace. He turned and glowered at Hubert. Hubert wasn't intimidated. The lanky teen shook the basket of fries, then took out a pair of sunglasses from his shirt pocket and put them on.

"Whoa, boss," Hubert said with a grin, holding up his hands. "Total eclipse of the sun, dude!"

Bob took out his yacht captain's hat and placed it on his head. "That better?" he asked Hubert.

Hubert laughed. "Sure, boss."

Captain Bob smiled and turned back to the cash register.

"Hey, homey," Trey whispered to Bob. "Are you going to let him get away with that?"

Bob smiled. "Old Chinese saying: Let your enemy think he has defeated you, and then destroy him."

"What does that mean?"

"That means that Hubert better sleep with both eyes open. I've got a special surprise for him."

Trey laughed. "Groovy. I thought maybe Herr Frankenstein's computer had damaged your brain." He turned and walked back to the walk-in refrigerator.

Bob turned to the grill and the frying burgers. Trey's idle comment had brought back the recent battle with the infamous Herr Henry Frankenstein and his hunchbacked assistant, Fritz. Captain Bob and his friends had come close to losing their lives. With the first two monsters, Nina, Joe, and Bob had to merely track down the monsters and then destroy them by returning each to his respective movie. But with Herr Frankenstein, the teens became the hunted as the mad scientist attempted to create his monster using Trey, Joe, Captain Bob, and a senior named Oscar Morales as body parts. Ironically, it was the original Frankenstein monster who had saved Bob and his friends as the monster attacked its creator. When all was said and done, the monster, Herr Frankenstein, and Fritz were all transported back into the classic horror show from which they had escaped.

The mad scientist had wanted to steal Trey's and Bob's brains to endow his new creation with extraordinary mental powers. Herr Frankenstein had shaved the heads of the two freshmen in preparation for the operation.

Bob flipped the burgers and pressed on the patties with the spatula. He and the others knew they had three more monsters to fight. The digital video camera that Joe had modified had not worked on Frankenstein. With Count Dracula, the camera had vacuumed in the vampire like so much lint. With the Wolf Man, the camera plus a little hocus-pocus from a shaman's dream catcher had returned the werewolf to his classic movie. However, with Frankenstein, the camera had failed completely. Only when Joe sat at the mad scientist's computer and began typing in the special 3-D DVD code to mix with the DNA code were

Frankenstein, Fritz, and the monster transported back into the sad tale of *Frankenstein*.

If the camera no longer works, Bob thought, *how are we going to defeat the last three monsters?*

"Hey, buddy!"

Captain Bob started and spun around, inadvertently flinging burger grease into the air.

"Hey!" Hubert shouted as the grease hit his shirt. "This is my favorite shirt!"

"Why so jumpy?" Joe Motley stood in front of the cash register, his fingers drumming the top of the machine.

"Just thinking about Frankenstein," Bob said.

"Oh," Joe said knowingly. "Well, just put those memories in your freshman year scrapbook. We've got a new problem."

"What?" Bob said, although he had a feeling he knew what his best friend was about to say.

"Imhotep, the Mummy, is in town."

CHAPTER TWO
Saturday, 11 A.M.
Convention Center

"I'm sorry, but Professor Tovar was called away on urgent business at the university," Karl Homer was saying. "I'm going to be in charge until he returns."

"When will that be?" Nina asked. She was disappointed. She had read both of Professor Tovar's books on Egyptian antiquities and had looked forward to asking him about his discoveries.

"I'm not sure," Homer replied. He pulled a piece of paper from his pocket and unfolded it. "The telegram says that he is needed at the University of West Florida, and that I should take charge. That's all." He put the paper back into his pocket.

"Does that mean we can all go home and go back to bed?" Stacy said with a large yawn.

The students from Ponce High were sitting in the auditorium of the convention center, a semicircular theater in which the seats rose from the floor and looked down onto a small stage.

"No," Homer said. "That means that I'm in charge. I met with your humanities teacher yesterday and explained the situation to her." He picked up a clipboard and scanned the list. "Mrs. Hoving has placed you in pairs to work with one of Professor Tovar's graduate assistants. I'll call out your names and the GA that will be in charge of you. You will then meet with your GA and let him or her explain your duties. I know some of you are here because you need the extra credit in school and some are here because you have an interest in archaeology. Let me remind you that you are responsible for anything you break."

"Like anything this old could be worth something," Stacy muttered.

Homer frowned at her. Then he began reading off the names.

"I hope I get a female GA," Angela whispered to Nina. "The way things are with Todd and me, I don't need some college guy hitting on me."

Nina nodded absentmindedly. She looked at the five GAs. She was excited about working with real college students. She hoped that she got a GA who wasn't just another geeky boy, but one with brains and looks and a sense of humor. Three of the GAs were guys and the other two were girls. Two of the guys were kind of cute — not Brendan Fraser cute, but cute enough. The other one looked as though he had stepped out of *GQ — Geek Quarterly* — and Nina sent up a silent prayer to the dating god that she wouldn't be placed with him. She really was tired of hanging around with pocket-protector boys.

"Marvin Sleaman," Homer called out.

Nina moaned inwardly as the poster boy for high-water pants stood up. Even his name was geeky.

Please, please, please, please, Nina prayed.

"Angela Chavarria and Jason Shippnick."

"Thank goodness," Nina said out loud.

"Yeah, thanks," Angela said with a frown. "See you after lunch." She scooted down the aisle and joined Jason and the GA in a corner of the auditorium.

"Hannah Tucker," Homer called out.

Nina looked around, but neither of the two girl GAs stood up. Perhaps Angela was right: better to get a girl and forget about boys. After all, they weren't there to flirt; they were there to learn.

Then Nina saw a small head bobbing between the aisles. A puzzled look crossed her face. Then a young girl emerged from the aisles and walked down next to Homer.

"This is Hannah Tucker," Homer explained.

"She's only twelve years old but she already has two degrees: one in ancient languages and a second in anthropology. Don't let her age or her size fool you. She's what we call a prodigy." Homer looked down at his clipboard.

"Oh, yes, the two newcomers: Joe Motley and Robert Hardin."

Nina gasped and looked around. Three rows behind her were Joe and Bob.

"How do you do?" Bob said, tipping his hat.

"Hey," Joe said.

"What are you two doing here?" Nina said, stunned.

"Ask Mr. Let's-Get-Up-at-Sunrise," Bob said with a glower toward his best friend.

"I tried to call you last night, but your line was busy," Joe said.

"I was talking to Angela," Nina explained.

"I've got to be at work by two," Bob said. "So I ain't sticking around all day."

"What did you want to talk about?" Nina said.

"Well —" Joe began.

"You two want to join me before I reach my sixteenth birthday?" came a high-pitched voice.

Joe and Bob looked down at the stage. Hannah had her hands on her hips and a scowl on her face. Her hair was pulled back into braided pigtails and a pair of bright pink-framed glasses highlighted her freckled face.

"Uh, yeah, sure," Joe said, jumping up.

"This is gonna be fun," Bob said through gritted teeth.

"You knew the job was dangerous when you took it," Nina replied with a smile.

"I didn't take the job. Big Boy here made me come. I'd rather be home in bed on a Saturday morning." Bob squeezed between the rows of seats and joined Joe. They walked down the aisle toward the pint-sized genius. "I'm off, said the madman," Bob growled, waving at Nina.

When all the Ponce students and GAs were matched up, Nina found that she and Stacy were left alone in the audience. Homer was stuffing his briefcase with a pile of papers. He snapped the case shut and prepared to leave.

"Mr. Homer," Nina said, raising her hand. "Who are we working with?"

"Oh, yes," Homer said as he walked up the aisle toward the two girls. "You'll be working with Levi Tovar. He's in the Egyptian room. Follow me."

"Is Levi Tovar related to Professor Tovar?" Nina asked as the two girls followed.

"He's Professor Tovar's son," Homer replied.

The girls followed Homer out of the auditorium and down the hallway.

"What a waste of a good Saturday," Stacy complained as she brought up the rear. "This is the first Saturday in weeks it hasn't been stormy. And I get stuck with *you*."

"Look, Stacy," Nina said, slowing down, "this is important to me. Let's be honest: I don't need the grade, but you do, okay? You just go along with whatever we have to do, and I'll help you through it. You'll get your grade."

"And what do you get?"

"I get to learn."

Stacy smiled. "You're getting the raw end of the deal, Nerd Girl." Stacy walked a few more feet, thinking. "Okay, but I don't do windows or heavy lifting."

"Whatever. Just don't call me Nerd Girl again or the deal's off and you fail humanities."

Stacy's face scrunched up in a frown. "You want to take all the fun out of this, don't you?"

Nina ignored her.

"Okay: deal. But I don't want it getting around that you and I are friends. We can be civil, but after this thing is over, you're a stranger to me."

"Whatever," Nina replied, rolling her eyes.

"This is Levi Tovar," Homer said as he and the girls entered the Egyptian room.

Nina looked around but didn't see anybody. Then she heard a noise behind the sarcophagus, a grating sound, like two stones being rubbed together.

"Levi," Homer called out.

The young man sprang up from behind the sarcophagus so suddenly that both girls yelped.

"What?" Homer said, turning sharply to look at the girls.

"Nothing," Nina said. "He just scared us, that's all."

"Yeah," Stacy added, annoyed. "I mean, like, we're in a room with a coffin and a dead body and he jumps out like it's Halloween or something."

"Sarcophagus," the young man said.

"What?" Stacy said, still annoyed.

"It's not a coffin; it's a sarcophagus." Levi Tovar crossed toward them.

"What's the diff? They both have dead people in them," Stacy said, one hand on her hip.

"True," Levi said. He was wiping a fine gray dust from his hands with a soiled rag. His face was covered with it, as was his black hair. "And you're right, in a way. A coffin does hold people. Common people. Ordinary people. People like you and me. But a sarcophagus holds queens and kings and pharaohs and those who aspire to be gods."

"Maybe *you're* common, but —" Stacy began, but the young man cut her off.

"I'm Levi Tovar," he announced, thrusting his hand toward Nina.

"Nina," Nina said.

Even with dust covering his face, Nina could tell that Levi was cute. And he squeezed her hand before releasing it.

"Stacy McDonald," Stacy said, grabbing Levi's hand. "Ooh," she cried out, jerking her hand away. "What have you been doing? Playing in dirt?" Stacy's right hand was covered in the same fine gray dust that coated Levi.

"Oh, sorry," Levi said, and he began wiping her hand with his rag.

"No way," Stacy said. She took a tissue from her purse and wiped off her hand.

"Just what were you doing?" Homer asked.

"I was trying to get Ptah-Soker-Osiris open," Levi explained.

"Pa-tah-Soaker-What-Is?" Stacy asked as she finished wiping her hand clean.

"The Ptah-Soker-Osiris," Nina said. Levi looked at her, surprised. "Wooden figurines that were sometimes used to hide papyrus scrolls with excerpts from the *Book of the Dead*."

Levi whistled. "Have I died and met Isis?"

"The book of the what?" Stacy said.

"The *Book of the Dead*," Levi said. Then he looked at Nina. "Go on."

"The *Book of the Dead*," she began, hesitating a little, "contained the funerary rights for the ancient Egyptians. Without it, the immortal soul had no hope of spending eternity with

Osiris. Some kept excerpts in wooden figurines of themselves in the hope that this would please Osiris and win them special favors in the underworld."

Levi looked at Homer. "I think I'll keep her."

"Sounds like a bunch of mumbo jumbo to me," Stacy said. "Where's the trash can?"

Levi grabbed the tissue. "I'll take care of this."

"I've got work to do," Homer announced and left the room.

"Where'd you learn all that?" Levi said.

"Some in class," Nina answered. "Plus I read up on the exhibit when I learned it was coming to San Tomas."

"Yeah," Stacy said with a sarcastic smile. "She has no life, so she reads about dead things."

Nina shot Stacy a glare. "Some of us work hard for our *grades*."

Stacy frowned and remained silent.

"Hey, more power to you," Levi said. "I'm glad to have someone to work with who knows something about Egyptology besides what they've learned in horror movies. You'd be surprised," Levi said to Nina as he returned to the other side of the sarcophagus. "Some students can't tell their Ka from their Ba."

Stacy frowned.

"Never mind — it won't be on the test. Just laugh," Nina told her.

Stacy giggled and then frowned when she realized Nina was talking down to her.

Levi bent down behind the stone sarcophagus and then straightened up again. In his hands was a wooden image like the one of the mummy that lay in the stone tomb.

"This is a wooden model of our queen," Levi said. He placed the wooden figurine on top of the sarcophagus. It was in every way an exact replica of the mummy casing inside the stone tomb. "Dad was particularly lucky to find this along with the other treasures."

"Why?" Stacy said.

"Most of the tombs were raided by robbers and the gold was stolen, along with jewels and anything else of value," Nina explained.

"That's right," Levi said with a smile.

Stacy rolled her eyes.

"What happened to Hapy?" Nina said, picking up a shard from a broken canopic jar.

"I don't know," Levi said in a whisper. "And I don't want to be around when my father finds out." He walked over to the table and began trying to piece the clay shards together. "It's rare to find all the canopic jars intact. Someone must have broken this one setting up the exhibit. Dad's going to go through the roof when he gets back and finds this."

"What are *those*?" Stacy said as she joined the pair.

"Canopic jars held the entrails of the dead," Levi explained. "Each jar represents one of the sons of Horus: the man head is Imset. He guarded the liver. The falcon-headed guardian is Qebhesnuef, and he protected the intestines. And Duametef here" — he picked up the jackal-headed jar — "had the honor of protecting the stomach."

"And that one?" Stacy said, pointing to the broken jar.

"That's Hapy. He protected the lungs," Levi said.

"Where's his head?" Stacy said.

Levi looked puzzled. Then he looked around the table. "Good question. Where is his head?"

Nina looked among the shards. "It's not here. At least none of the broken pieces are here."

"Strange," Levi said.

"This whole thing is strange. Okay," Stacy said with a sigh, "what do we have to do?"

Levi shook his head and turned away from the table. "Let's get to work."

Four hours later, an exhausted Nina walked slowly down the hallway. Stacy walked beside her, humming.

"I don't think I've worked that hard in my life," Nina said.

"I know I haven't," Stacy replied.

"You didn't do anything except talk the whole time."

"I told you: I don't do windows and I don't do any heavy lifting. We have a deal, remember?"

"Our deal doesn't call for me to do everything. You've got to do something to earn your grade."

"Hey, I'm learning something. I know that Happy guards the guts and that Emmet has a yearning for the liver, and Tweedledum and Tweedledee guard the stomach and lungs."

Nina rolled her eyes. "It's a good thing none of this is going to be on the test. You could have at least helped me move that stone lid on the sarcophagus."

"I'm not touching anything that's dead!"

"Perhaps you'd like to be dead yourself!" came a thunderous voice from behind them.

Stacy and Nina spun around.

A large man wearing an executioner's outfit and black mask lurched toward them, wielding a bloodstained ax at their heads.

CHAPTER THREE
Saturday Still
Beach Burger
5:30 P.M.

"That's one Beach Burger jumbo and one Beach Burger regular," Hubert said as he scribbled on the order pad. "Do you want fries with that?"

Captain Bob frowned as he pushed and pulled the large slicing machine back and forth, shreds of lettuce falling into a large red plastic bowl. All Beach Burger hamburgers came with french fries. Hubert had worked at the popular beachside hamburger restaurant almost six months and still didn't know the menu. Bob was glad that Trey was working at the Beach Burger now, too. At least time seemed to fly when Trey was working with him. Not only that, Bob's school grades had begun to improve with Trey's tutelage, and Bob's mother was thinking about letting him back on his computer.

Bob had protested to his mother that he needed his computer to study. She had replied that he would have to study the old-fashioned way — by taking notes. Bob had protested further until his mother threatened to sell his computer. Bob had to give in then — it was his most prized possession.

Bob finished the head of lettuce, cleaned off the machine, and threw the lettuce that had fallen on the preparation table into the trash. Although he didn't like working on Saturdays, he was glad his mom had scheduled him this week. If he had spent one more hour with Hannah Tucker and her whiny know-it-all voice, he would have gone insane. Being a madman was one thing; being insane was quite another.

Joe had just better appreciate his friendship. Not many friends would give up a Saturday morning of sleep to volunteer to work for a humanities exhibition. Joe had convinced him, however, that the fourth of the deadly monsters they had released would appear soon. What better place than an Egyptian exhibition with a real petrified queen for the Mummy to appear?

Bob had secretly hoped that the Bride of Frankenstein would appear next. He wouldn't admit this to anyone, not even his best friend, but Bob thought that the Bride of Frankenstein was kind of hot. She had a perky little nose and nice large lips. Her eyes would make Katie Holmes envious. So what if she had hair like

Marge Simpson and had been pieced together from various parts of other women? Perhaps that was the best way to find a nice girl, Bob thought. Make your own.

He picked up the red bowl and started toward the cooler when a strong hand grabbed his right shoulder.

"Yeow!" Bob yelled, losing his grip on the bowl of freshly shredded lettuce. It flew into the air. Bob spun around.

Joe's head and shoulders were draped in strands of lettuce. Joe frowned and began pulling it out of his hair. Nina stood behind him, stifling a giggle.

"Hey, why are you so jumpy lately?" Joe said, dropping the lettuce to the floor. "You're usually not afraid of anything."

"I know. And I don't know," Bob said, helping his friend with the lettuce. "I guess our battle with Frankenstein really got to me. I can't walk past a mirror without jumping at my own reflection."

"Now you know how the rest of us feel," Nina put in. She grabbed a broom and began sweeping up the lettuce.

"Thanks," Bob sneered.

"You're welcome," Nina said.

"Hey, where'd you get that?" Bob said, noticing the black-and-blue half-moon under Joe's left eye.

"Let's just say it's the tail end of a good joke gone bad," Joe said, brushing the last of the lettuce from his shoulder.

"What?" Bob said, perplexed.

"Joe thought he'd play a practical joke and dress up like a medieval executioner," Nina explained. "He played his part well."

"Too well," Joe said.

"You let Nina give you a black eye?" Bob asked incredulously.

"That's the least I would have done if I had gotten ahold of him," Nina said.

"No, she didn't do it," Joe said. "He did." Joe nodded toward the lobby area of the restaurant to a booth against one wall. Sitting at the booth was Levi Tovar. "He heard the girls scream, ran up behind me, and punched me in the eye."

"A sucker punch," Bob exclaimed.

"Joe was a sucker for pulling a stunt like that," Nina replied.

"I was just getting into character," Joe explained.

"What?" Bob said.

"We get to dress up in the period we're working in at the opening of the exhibit," Joe said. "I get to be an executioner."

"What about me?" Bob said. "What do I get to dress up as?"

"You should have stuck around, buddy," Joe

said, his voice low. "Hannah assigned you the jester costume."

Bob groaned. "I really don't like that little girl."

"I'm not a little girl!" came a shrill voice from behind Joe.

Bob peeked around his large friend. Hannah was glaring at him. She turned, stomped over to a table, and sat across from Angela and Marvin. Marvin had a big smile on his face, and Angela looked uncomfortable.

"Great," Bob murmured. Then he said to Joe, "What did you do, bring the whole crew down here?"

"The Atomic Drive-in is still undergoing renovations," Nina explained. "The gang wanted some good food, and the Beach Burger is the next best thing."

"Just remember," Bob said, nodding toward the jar.

"I know. I know," Nina said. "Tipping isn't the capital of China. When are you going to get rid of that corny jar?"

"When it's full," Bob replied.

"I'll fill it —" Nina began.

"With money," Bob blurted. "Hey, Hubert, I'm going on break," he called over his shoulder, taking off his name tag and thrusting it in his pocket.

"We don't get breaks," Hubert said.

Bob ignored his coworker and followed Joe to the booth. Nina sat next to Levi, leaving Bob and Joe the seat across from them.

Hubert made the rounds, taking orders, and soon everyone was munching on hamburgers and fries.

"When do you think your father will be back?" Nina asked Levi.

"Hard to say. It's really not that unusual for him to have to return to the university to take care of business. He ought to retire, but he's afraid they'll put in someone who doesn't care as much about the work as he does."

"I think the exhibition is a great idea," Nina said.

"My father thought it up a few years ago. He's afraid that interest in archaeology will die. He's hoping the traveling show will encourage teenagers to pursue careers in archaeology."

"Yeah," Joe said between bites. "Everyone thinks it's like *Indiana Jones* or something."

"Exactly," Levi agreed. "It's long, hard work and often boring."

"Like school," Bob chimed in, slurping down the last of his soft drink.

"Not exactly," Levi said. "School's a piece of cake compared to digging in the desert, where it's one hundred and ten in the shade."

"What I don't understand," Nina began, "is why you and Bob here volunteered. Both of you told me last week you'd rather swallow live goldfish than work at the exhibition."

"I didn't volunteer," Bob said.

"That's what we want to talk to you about," Joe said. "But later." He tried not to act suspicious, but he felt his face flush as he avoided Levi's eyes.

"Okay," Nina said. "But make it tomorrow. I'm going to help Levi with the exhibition some more tonight."

"Tonight?" Bob blurted. "That was quick."

"What do you mean by that?" Nina shot back.

"Nothing," Bob said, poking out his lower lip.

"We really need to talk to you, Nina," Joe said.

"You can come help me tomorrow, Nina," Levi said. "I don't want to interfere with what you and your friends have going on."

"We have *nothing* going on," Nina said in protest.

"It's important, Nina," Joe said, his eyes pleading.

Nina mentally kicked herself. She was about to cancel time alone with the first promising guy she'd met all year because two freshmen boys wanted to talk with her. Two freshmen boys who had brought her nothing but trouble since the day she met them.

"What's wrong with you?" Bob said loudly, eyeing Levi.

Nina turned. Levi's face had reddened. Sweat poured down his forehead. His lips trembled. His breathing was shallow.

"Levi?" Nina said, concern in her voice.

Levi leaned back in the booth and tilted his head back. His eyes rolled back.

"Levi!" Nina began to pound on his back, thinking that something was lodged in his throat.

Levi's head tilted downward. The red slowly seeped from his face. He blinked his eyes and then shook his head.

"I'm okay," he said breathlessly. "I'm okay."

"What happened?" Nina said softly. Her eyes were tender.

Oh, brother, Bob thought.

"What happened?" Nina repeated.

"I'm okay," Levi said again.

"He's got claustrophobia," Marvin explained, walking up to the table. "He gets this way if he feels like the walls are closing in on him."

"Or someone's sitting too close to him," Bob said.

Nina glared at him.

"I'm okay," Levi said. "I just couldn't breathe. Felt like everything was swimming around me."

"I'll take him back to the motel," Marvin said.

"Yes," Levi said. "I need to get out in the open for a while."

"I'll give you a ride," Nina said, scooting out of the booth.

"No," Levi said, swallowing hard. "You stay with your friends. I'll be okay. Marvin can get me to the motel room." Marvin helped Levi stand and the pair started toward the door.

"C'mon, Hannah," Marvin said, and he and Levi disappeared into the early evening.

Hannah stood up and looked directly at Bob. "Don't be late tomorrow."

"*Sieg heil*," Bob said and then stuck his tongue out at her. Hannah returned the gesture.

"I think she likes you," Joe said with a smile.

"Thanks a lot, Joe." Nina kicked Joe under the table.

"Ouch! What was that for?"

"You blew her big chance with Dream Boy," Bob said, smiling.

"It wasn't like that," Nina protested.

"You're all over him like a puppy with a new toy," Bob said.

"One of these days, Bob, I'm going to get mad and just slap your face. Every time I get close to a guy, you come along and belch or pass gas or do some stupid freshman thing, and now every guy at school thinks I'm just some geeky girl who hangs around with freshmen creeps!"

"Does that include me?" Joe said, looking hurt.

"You two are a pair of flies on my birthday cake."

"Don't blame me if you can't get a boyfriend!" Bob smirked.

"I blame you for everything that's happened since the day I met you!"

"Yeah? Well, my life hasn't been a barrel of monkeys since I met you!"

"All right," Joe said, his voice low. "We can sit around here blame-storming, or we can start thinking about how to capture the next monster."

There was pain and anger in Nina's eyes. She had been angry and upset at Bob more than once since they had met the previous June, but she had never been so infuriated with the short freshman as she was at this moment. Why was this time different? Could it be that she really liked Levi? Or was it that Bob had finally yanked her chain once too often? She didn't like being out of control emotionally.

Bob sat silently, his eyes staring past the plate of cold fries and half-eaten burger. He had never seen Nina this upset, not even when he had put fake barf on the floorboard of her Camaro. Something was different this time. Bob couldn't quite put his finger on it, but something was different. Without really trying, he had gotten so far under Nina's skin that she was ready to throttle him.

"Okay," Joe finally said. "Peace?" He looked at Nina and then at Bob.

"Peace," Bob said.

Nina took longer to say it, but she finally relented. "Peace."

"Can I join you?" Angela said, appearing at Nina's side.

"Yeah," Nina said. She smiled, glad to have her friend there to ease the tension. She scooted over in the booth, and Angela sat down.

"I wasn't sure," Angela said. "I thought a nuclear war had broken out over here."

"Let's just forget it," Bob said, still staring at his plate.

"What is so important, Joe?" Nina stared at the large freshman.

"Bob and I are convinced that the fourth monster has appeared."

"Really?" Angela said, excitement in her voice.

"Really," Bob said, mocking Angela.

Nina glared at Bob. "Which one?" she asked.

"Imhotep, the Mummy," Joe replied. "I'm surprised you didn't think of it."

"Think of what?" Nina said.

"The Egyptian exhibition with the mummified queen. It's just what the Mummy would be looking for," Joe explained.

Nina frowned. "Yeah, I thought about it, but then dismissed it."

"Why?" Bob said. His voice was calm, and the color had returned to his face. "Why did you dismiss it?"

"It's too much of a coincidence," Nina said. "It's too easy. We have a Western Civilization exhibit that just happens to have a mummified Egyptian queen. It's like the Mummy is just begging us to stop him. In fact, I was going to talk to you guys about the next monster." She pulled a folded sheet of paper from her pocket. "I got this off that weird site you like to visit, Bob. I'm surprised you didn't find it."

"I'm grounded from the computer until my grades come up," Bob explained.

Nina was tempted to say something sarcastic about Bob and his grades, but she bit her tongue. She didn't want another fight.

"I think it's the Creature from the Black Lagoon." She unfolded the paper and set it in between Bob and Joe. She turned to Angela. "It's a story from that crazy site Bob visits, the one with the stories about two-headed people and werewolves and stuff. Two fishermen were attacked and killed last week while they were fishing near the NASA Causeway."

"That's just ten miles south of here," Angela said.

"Right," Nina confirmed. "The authorities claim that a great white shark is on the loose."

"There's never been a great white in this area," Angela said.

"Correct. Witnesses, however, have told the tabloids and that weird Internet site that the two men were attacked by a giant fish that looked more like a man. In fact, the witnesses' descriptions fit the Gill Man from *Creature from the Black Lagoon* perfectly."

"You're right: It is the Creature from the Black Lagoon," Joe said as he looked up from the news copy. "But I don't think the Gill Man is our problem right now. Imhotep is right here in town."

"All right, let's say you're right. So let's review," Nina said. "In the original *The Mummy*, Imhotep comes to life when the archaeologist who discovered him reads aloud to himself from a magical papyrus. Imhotep is then transformed into the Egyptologist Ardeth Bey, who discovers ten years later that the spirit of his long-lost love resides in the body of Helen Grosvenor."

"That sounds too much like *Dracula*," Angela said with a shudder, remembering her encounter with the fiendish bloodsucker.

"Bob?" Joe turned to his friend.

Bob was sitting back in the booth, listening

to Nina. He was surprised at her detailed knowledge of *The Mummy*. Usually it was Bob who provided the group with the minute facts from the old films that gave them clues to the discovery of the monsters.

"She's right about the movie," Bob said. "Plus, in the movie, Imhotep's long-lost love is a princess, not a queen."

Nina looked at Bob. He smiled slightly, and she smiled back at him. "Okay," she continued. "So in order for Imhotep to appear, there have to be two mummies: one for Imhotep, and one for his dead lover. We've got a queen that Professor Tovar had discovered in the Valley of the Kings, but we don't have the second mummy, the one that becomes Imhotep." She sat back in the booth. "I went through the whole Egyptian exhibit. I was suspicious, too, and wanted to check it out myself. It's not the Mummy, Joe. It's the Gill Man, and he's attacking people around the NASA Causeway."

Joe sat back, grabbed his soft drink, and took a big gulp. What Nina was saying made sense. While Captain Bob was ready to jump feetfirst into any sign of danger, Nina was more cautious and provided the group with the logic they needed to defeat the monsters. Whether or not the two would ever admit it, Nina and Bob were perfect complements for each other. When they put their heads and hearts together, the pair was nearly invincible. Joe smiled at the thought of Nina and Bob as a *couple*. Then he choked on his drink.

He cleared his throat and said, "I'm still not totally convinced." He turned to Bob. "You remember Skylar Crockett?"

"Crazy Crockett? The guy who can make wallets out of duct tape?" Bob said, raising his eyebrows.

"Yeah, him. He lives down near the causeway. I'll call him and see if he knows anything." He looked at Nina. "Okay?"

Nina nodded.

"But I think we're wasting time."

Nina frowned. "Let's go," she said to Angela. "I'll drop you off at home."

"Actually, I have to go back to the convention center," Angela said, grimacing. "Marvin wants his group to do some more work on the medieval exhibit."

"Sounds like a fun date," Nina said, raising her eyebrows.

Angela crossed her eyes, stuck a finger in her mouth, and pretended to gag.

"I'm going to walk home," Joe announced. "I need time to think."

"Okay, see you at the convention center tomorrow," Nina said, and she and Angela left the Beach Burger together.

"Hey," Bob said. "How about letting me out?"

"Huh?" Joe said, lost in thought.

"Let me out," Bob repeated, pushing on his friend's shoulder.

Joe scooted out of the booth. Bob followed him.

"I've got to stay until closing and clean up. Want to hang around?" Bob took his captain's hat from his back pocket and flipped it onto the top of his head.

"No," Joe said. "I've got to get home. I'll see you tomorrow."

"Later," Bob said, disappearing behind the counter.

Joe walked out of the Beach Burger. The winter wind greeted him with a cold embrace, and he zipped up his black leather jacket and pulled the collar around his neck. The leather strained around Joe's large, muscular body. He'd only had the jacket since the summer and already he was growing out of it. Being fourteen was tough. And being fourteen, six-foot-one, and still growing was a nightmare sometimes. Bob got picked on because he was short, and Joe was hassled because he was so tall. Sometimes Joe wished he were all grown up already.

It was only six-thirty, but darkness had set on San Tomas Inlet. Joe turned left on Beach Front Road and headed toward home. He longed for spring, when he could run up and down the beach in his shorts and his favorite Hawaiian shirt.

Joe was so lost in thought he failed to notice the black van sitting in the alley — and the creature that stepped out of it.

A steely grip squeezed Joe's shoulder. He spun around and found himself staring into the hollow eye sockets and dead, expressionless face of a mummy. Part of Joe wanted to shout, "See! I told you so!" but the mummy didn't give him time to celebrate. It swung with its free arm and caught Joe on the right temple. Joe's legs began to buckle beneath him.

Joe grabbed the mummy as he slid to the ground, but the mummy's wrappings ripped from the creature and pieces of rotten flesh came off in Joe's hands. His knees hit the concrete with a fleshy thud. Joe leaned back, balled up his right hand, and landed a solid jab to the mummy's stomach. His fist went through the ancient wrappings and the dried flesh like a steel pole through paper. His arm was embedded in the mummy's stomach up to his elbow. The mummy grunted, grabbed Joe in a headlock, and began dragging the teen to the black van. Joe squirmed to free his head, but the mummy held Joe in the crook of his arm like a vise. With his arm protruding out through the mummy's back, Joe began tearing the ancient cloth wrapping.

The mummy threw Joe through the open rear van doors. Joe hit the metal floor, and the breath was knocked out of him. Dazed, he watched as the mummy climbed into the van and shut the doors. Joe tried to sit up, but the mummy slapped him on the forehead with the palm of his hand. It felt like a sledgehammer crashing into his skull.

Joe groaned and fell back to the van's floor.

"Very good, my faithful servant," came a voice from the front of the van. Joe tilted his head and strained to see the speaker. A dim red light lit the interior of the van. "You have done well." The speaker was shrouded in blackness against the dim red light. Joe squirmed, but was able to move very little. He tried to focus his eyes. The man's body appeared normal, but his head was oddly shaped, conical but ending in a smooth, flat top.

The silhouette moved from the front seat to the rear of the van. Joe followed the man's hands and saw them reach into a plastic bag hanging from a hook on the side of the van. Through the dimness of his swimming mind, Joe recognized it as an IV bag.

The man unhooked the needle from the bag and lowered it to Joe's neck. Then the dark man turned his head upward and spoke in a deep voice:

"Oh! Amon-Ra — Oh! God of gods — Death is but the doorway to a new life — We live today — We shall live again — In many forms shall we return — Oh, Mighty One."

The dark man began pressing the needle into Joe's flesh. "You'll feel a little sting," the man said. "And then you'll feel nothing at all."

CHAPTER FOUR

Just then, red and blue lights flooded the inside of the van. Startled, the man dropped the needle and jumped into the driver's seat. The engine of the van roared to life as the man slammed the shift lever down, and the van lurched forward.

Then Joe heard the familiar wail of a police siren. The shrill sound helped snap Joe out of his stupor. He sat up. The mummy swung a rotten arm at Joe's head, but Joe ducked, and only gray dust hit him this time.

The mummy jumped forward, wrapping his arms around the large teenager. Joe stood, stooping over in the van, and he and the mummy grappled for an advantage. The driver turned the steering wheel wildly to the left and right, and the combatants caromed off the sides of the van as the vehicle tilted first one way and then the other.

Ancient dust filled the air, and Joe found

breathing difficult. The van suddenly spun sharply to the left, and the mummy slammed into the side of the van. Joe sprang at the mummy and put the creature into a headlock.

The mummy struggled against Joe, turning its head one way and then the next. Joe squeezed harder. He knew that he couldn't suffocate the dead creature — after all, the dead don't breathe — but he hoped he could hang on to the mummy long enough for the police to stop the mad driver.

The mummy continued to squirm. Then Joe suddenly heaved forward. The mummy was free. Or at least, its body was free. Its head was still in the crook of Joe's right arm. Joe yelled, dropped the head, and kicked it to the front of the van. He turned in time to see the headless body of the mummy pitch toward him, its arms flailing the air in a mad attempt to grab on to anything. Joe pushed against the mummy's chest, trying to keep the thing from grabbing him. With a power and determination all their own, the mummy's arms thrashed the air, hitting Joe about the face and shoulders, filling the air with ancient gray dust. Joe coughed and tried to breathe through the airborne filth.

The driver continued on his reckless path, throwing Joe and the headless mummy around the back of the van. The van turned sharply to the left and Joe and the mummy soared to the back of the van, slamming so hard against the doors that they flew open. Joe and the headless mummy sailed through the air and slammed into the ground, Joe landing on top. The long-dead mummy instantly disintegrated into a cloud of dust.

Joe looked up in wide-eyed terror as the headlights of the police cruiser bore down on him. He threw his arms up over his head and gritted his teeth against the inevitable.

There was a screech of tires as the patrol car screamed to a halt inches from Joe's head.

Joe dropped his arms and took a deep breath.

"Don't move!" came a gruff command. "Put your hands behind your head and get to your knees."

Joe did as he was told, squinting in the bright headlights of the patrol car.

"Don't I know you?" the voice said sternly.

Joe coughed. "My name is Joe Motley. I'm a freshman at the high school."

"You're one of Detective Turner's kids, aren't you?"

"Yes," Joe said.

"I'm Officer Elliott. What were you doing in that van?"

"Trying to escape."

"Escape?"

"Yeah. Some senior guys grabbed me. Some

sort of upperclassman joke." Joe decided not to tell the police officer about the mummy or the man with the needle.

"Okay," the officer said. "Stand up." Joe stood and faced the officer. "Jeez, you're a big fella. You play football for the high school? I'm a big Bulldog fan."

"No," Joe said, brushing the dust from his leather jacket and pants.

"You hurt anywhere?"

"No." He pulled a piece of ancient wrapping from his forehead and looked at it. Only it wasn't a patch of ancient wrapping, it was a swath of mummified skin. Joe gingerly put it in his jacket pocket to examine later.

"Looks like they got away," the officer said, tipping his hat back and looking in the direction in which the van had disappeared. "Let's get you to the station and call your parents."

"Thanks."

"Did you get a look at the guy?" Detective Turner said as he handed Joe a cup of water.

"It was too dark," Joe replied. He sipped the water slowly. "He had a funny-looking head, though. Like a cone, only flat on top."

"Like a conehead?" said Officer Elliott.

"Listen, Officer Elliott." Turner put his arm on the officer's shoulder and walked him toward his office door. "Why don't you wait until Joe's parents arrive and then escort them back here to my office. Okay?" Turner smiled.

"Sure, Detective." Elliott looked at Joe. "I'm glad you're okay, kid. The Bulldogs need players like you if we're gonna win district next year."

Turner shut the door and faced Joe. "Okay: Tell me what you couldn't tell me when Elliott was in here." He folded his arms across his chest.

Joe smiled a little. Detective Turner tried to strike an imposing stance, but the small detective looked more like a kid in a school play than one of San Tomas Inlet's best detectives.

"Imhotep, the Mummy, is in town," Joe said without emotion.

"Uh-huh," Turner replied. He sat at his desk and swung his feet up on top of it. "Another one of your movie monsters?" Turner laughed.

"You wouldn't think it so funny if he had tried to drain your blood."

Turner sat up. "Drain your blood?"

"Yeah. He was about to put a needle in my neck."

Turner picked up a folder from the top of his desk. "Are you sure it's the Mummy? Could Count Dracula be back in town?"

"Why do you ask?" Joe said, his face scrunching up.

"This doesn't leave this office," Turner said with a knowing look at Joe. "We found a body on the beach last night drained of blood. There was a puncture mark in his neck." He handed the folder to Joe. "If I hadn't helped you fight Frankenstein, I'd say you were crazy."

Joe glanced through the police report and the photos of the dead man, then he handed the folder back to Turner.

"Either it was the same men who attacked you tonight, or we've got a one-fanged vampire on the loose."

"It can't be Count Dracula," Joe said.

"Why not?" Turner leaned back in his chair. "Isn't that how all of this started five months ago — with bloodless bodies showing up?"

"Yeah," Joe confirmed. "But Dr. Dunn, I mean Count Dracula, is back in his movie. You saw it yourself after we watched *Frankenstein*. Remember?"

Turner frowned. "Yeah." He scratched his nose. "You think the Egyptian exhibit at the convention center has something to do with the appearance of Imhotep?"

"Yeah, but Nina almost had me convinced that the Gill Man was here instead."

"Why?"

Joe pulled out the printed Internet report. Turner read it and handed it back to Joe. "We've heard about that. Local authorities say it's a shark."

"Local authorities in Volusia County said that the killings and mutilations there were the result of a cougar attack," Joe said. "Turned out it was the Wolf Man. Can't always rely on the local authorities." Joe smiled. "Present company excluded."

"Thanks," Turner replied with a wry smile. "You and Bob know I'm on your side. The rest may think you're just a couple of crazy teenagers, but then they didn't almost lose their hands to Herr Frankenstein and have to fight that ugly Fritz." Turner sipped cold coffee from a paper cup. He grimaced. He looked at Joe. "One more thing. If this really is Imhotep and he needs blood to keep living, why did he pick you?"

"Easy target?" Joe said with a half smile.

"No. There's got to be something else. The body we found on the beach was a large man as well."

Joe sighed. "I guess it's the season for hunting big guys."

"Just be careful."

Joe touched his forehead, right where he'd found the dried-out patch of skin. "Don't worry, I will."

CHAPTER FIVE
Monday, 12:30 p.m.
Lunchroom
Ponce de Leon High

Captain Bob Hardin sat at the cafeteria table, letting his oatmeal congeal. He had taken a couple of bites and decided he could do without the pasty oats for the day. He concentrated instead on what Joe was telling him. When Joe finished, Bob took another bite, then grimaced. It was cold. "So there were two of them," Bob said slowly. "Hmm. What about Levi and Marvin?"

"You think they have something to do with the Mummy?" Joe asked. "I mean the real Mummy, from the movie? They don't seem the types to be involved with monsters."

"Yeah, well, Dr. Thomas didn't appear to be Herr Frankenstein," Bob said with a smirk. "I'm going to keep an eye on Levi and Marvin."

"Whoever the real Mummy is, apparently he's using another mummy to do his bidding," Joe replied. He tapped the toast against his tray.

"This doesn't fit with the movie. And the

Mummy never needed blood in the movie. He turned into Ardeth Bey and waited ten years before finding the reincarnation of his lost love."

"I know. Oh, here's another thing — the guy in the van wore one of those cone-shaped hats, like those guys who ride the minibikes in the Christmas parade."

"A fez."

"Yeah, a fez."

The bell rang. Students hopped up from their seats and scurried toward the various exits leading to their classes.

"Let's see what the day brings," Captain Bob said, placing his yacht cap on his head.

"Let's see how long you stay out of trouble," Joe said as he pretended to set the stopwatch on his watch.

Bob frowned. "Some friend." Bob suddenly felt himself being pushed backward. Then he found himself on the floor.

"Oh, sorry," Levi said, looking down at Bob. He reached down his right hand. Bob took it and was quickly on his feet. "I wasn't watching where I was going."

A giggle erupted from behind Levi. Hannah Tucker peeked around the graduate assistant.

"Oh, brother," Bob groaned. "What are you two doing here?"

"I'm lecturing to Mrs. Hoving's humanities class," Levi replied.

"And I'm talking to Ms. Bashara's English class," the twelve-year-old prodigy responded.

Joe laughed.

"My day's shot," Bob said. "Nice pigtails," he said to the girl.

Hannah frowned and stomped her foot. "They're not pigtails, you small brain!"

"Yeah, yeah, yeah," Bob said as he walked away.

"You two were made for each other," Joe said, joining his friend.

"Like nitro and glycerin," Bob said.

2:15 P.M.
Mrs. Hoving's Humanities Class

"It's not what you see in the movies," Levi was saying. "Archaeology is long, hard, and often boring work. No leather jackets, wide-brim hats, or whips." Levi smiled.

Nina looked around the room. Some of the students were generally interested, some looked bored, and others looked as though they were in outer space. One student was asleep and drooling on the desk. Nina rolled her eyes. Then she saw Stacy McDonald staring at Levi. No, staring wasn't the right word. The right word was ogling. Yes, Stacy was ogling Levi.

"I've been on digs around the world, but the most exciting ones have been in Egypt," Levi continued. "The Egyptians were the first people to leave extensive records, not only about their daily lives but about their deaths as well. Other civilizations had written records, but nothing compared to the Egyptians. In fact, if you hate bureaucracy, you can blame it on the Egyptians."

A few students giggled. Stacy giggled just a little too loudly and a little too long. At least that's what Nina was thinking. Nina rolled her eyes and then raised her hand.

"Yes," Levi said.

"What do you think about—"

"I'm sorry, Nina. Stacy had her hand up first," Levi said with a soft smile.

Nina looked over at Stacy. Stacy's smile wasn't soft.

"I was just wondering about the makeup the Egyptians wore," Stacy said. "It seems like they just caked it on."

"Oh, brother," Nina muttered under her breath. Of all the questions that Stacy McDonald could have asked about the ancient Egyptians — about their engineering skills, their arts, their literature, their customs — she asked about fashion.

"That's a very good question," Levi said. Nina felt her face flush. "Once again, the Egyptians weren't the first people to use makeup, but they elevated it, as they did everything in their culture, to an art form. Makeup served two purposes: The first was practical; the second was aesthetic. Makeup helped to keep pesky insects from biting the Egyptians. The Egyptian makeup also acted as the first sunblock to help keep the skin from burning under the desert sun. But the Egyptians weren't just practical — they wanted to look good as well. Even the lowest slaves would be made up as best as they could afford — men and women. An Egyptian would never think of leaving home without looking her, or his, best."

"Yeah, unlike today," Stacy piped in, glancing at Nina. "Some people just don't know anything about fashion sense."

Nina sighed and did her best to ignore Stacy. She would love to come back with some sort of biting quip, but she didn't want to seem catty in front of Levi.

"The bell's about to ring," Mrs. Hoving said. She stood from behind her desk. "And for a nice little surprise."

Nina sat up.

"Before class began, Mr. Tovar told me that he would provide a free dinner to the student who asked the best question. I've been keeping track of the questions, and although they all were good, it seems that Stacy's question about the makeup not only covered an academic point but also a human-interest point. So Stacy gets the dinner."

Stacy squealed and her gaggle clapped.

Nina's face was red-hot.

The bell rang and the class emptied. Nina walked numbly from the room and into the hallway. She ignored Stacy and her group and headed for the exit leading to the student parking lot.

She was out the door and in the cool winter day when she heard someone calling her name.

"Nina!"

Nina turned. Levi walked quickly up to her.

"Where are you going? I've been calling you."

"Lost in thought," Nina said blandly.

"I'd say," Levi said. He put his arm around her shoulder. Nina shrugged it off. "Hey," he said softly.

"Hey, yourself," Nina said. Then her face flushed again as she realized how shrill her voice sounded.

"Whoa," Levi said, stopping. "What's up? I didn't mean anything by putting my arm around you. It just seemed natural."

Nina stopped beside her car. She unlocked the door, opened it, and threw her books inside. "Sorry," she said. She frowned. "I've never been jealous in my life." She bit her bottom lip. "So this is what it feels like."

"Jealous of what?" Levi said, perplexed. Then

he smiled. "Oooh. I didn't choose Stacy. Mrs. Hoving did."

"I know," Nina said. "That's why I'm confused about being jealous."

"Maybe you shouldn't analyze yourself so much," Levi said.

"I can't help it," Nina said. "I'm always trying to figure out why people do what they do, including myself. Captain Bob says I've got some real issues."

"Talk about someone with real issues," Levi said. "Captain Bob would drive Sigmund Freud crazy."

Nina snorted a laugh. Then her face flushed again. "Oh, sorry," she said, covering her mouth.

Levi placed his hands on her shoulders. Nina didn't shrug them away. "Don't be so hard on yourself. This may come as a shock to you, but you're human. You're going to be jealous and you're going to snort." He lifted her head with his right hand. "And I find that attractive."

Nina felt her legs melting as she stared into Levi's dark eyes. The cool winter wind danced between them. Nina felt herself moving slightly toward Levi. Levi leaned forward —

"Hey!" came a shout from the other side of Nina's car. "You know the chances of catching a cold from kissing in the middle of winter?"

Nina's eyes flared. She twisted her head. Captain Bob stood on the passenger side of the

Camaro, his head barely above the roof of the sports car, his lips in a wide "caught ya" smile. Joe stood next to Bob, leaning against the car, trying to be discreet.

"I'll see you at the convention center," Levi said. He squeezed her arm, turned, and headed back into the high school.

Nina hopped into the car and slammed the door behind her. Bob climbed in back and Joe slid in next to Nina.

Bob opened his mouth.

Nina glared at him in the rearview mirror. "Don't say a word, Bob." Her voice was low and threatening. "Not one word."

"What?" Bob said, genuinely confused.

"That's it," Nina said. "Out." She opened her door.

"Smooth move, Captain Boob," Joe said, trying not to laugh.

"What?" Bob said, still confused.

"Out!" Nina hopped out of the car and pushed the driver's seat forward.

Bob scooted out of the car. "What?"

Nina slammed her door, started the engine, and stomped on the accelerator. The tires squealed, and the car fishtailed as Nina guided it to the parking lot exit.

"What?" Bob said as he watched the car turn left on Beach Front Road. Then he shrugged. He'd better start walking. He had hoped Nina would drop him off at the Beach Burger. He looked at his watch. Walking would take him twenty minutes, and he'd be late. His mother would be angry with him. He was trying to get back on her good side, hoping she would let him use his computer again.

Now Nina was mad at him for some reason. All he had done was make a quip about kissing and colds, and Nina had turned on him like a pit bull. Everybody knew that he was a jokester. Joe kept telling him that he didn't know when to stop. Perhaps his friend was right.

A horn blared behind him, and Bob let out a yell. He spun around. Nina's white Camaro sat parked at the curb a few yards away. Joe smiled and waved from the passenger seat. Nina sat in the driver's seat, firing daggers at Bob with her eyes.

Joe opened his door, stood beside the car, and said, "Get in. Nina'll take you to work. But don't say a word."

Bob sighed and shrugged. He walked quickly to the passenger side and threw himself into the backseat.

Nina slowly moved away from the curb and into the lazy afternoon traffic.

"But what I don't understand," Nina said, as though continuing a conversation she and Joe were having before retrieving Bob, "is the whole blood business. That sounds more like Dracula than the Mummy."

Bob perked up. "Tha —"

"That's what Bob was saying this morning," Joe blurted out. "In the movie *The Mummy*, Imhotep tries to bring his love back to life, is found out, wrapped up, and then buried alive. A curse is placed on anybody who disturbs Imhotep's tomb."

"Then over three thousand years later, he's dug up, and he becomes Ardeth Bey," Nina added. "In a way, *The Mummy* is more of a love story. That's all Imhotep wanted: to be re-united with his love."

"The problem is," Joe said, "that in order to revive his love, he had to kill another woman."

"If that's true, then the Mummy is going to be after someone to kill to bring his love back," Nina said softly. "But who?"

"Just like with Dracula," Joe added just as softly.

"Joe, is the actress who played Dracula's love the same actress who played the Mummy's love?"

"No!" Bob blurted from the back. He sat forward. "I don't care if you kick me out of your car, Nina. I was only joking about the kiss. I'm sorry, okay?"

The car was silent. Joe looked at Nina. He

reached over, put his finger under her chin, and closed her mouth, which had been hanging open in shock. Then he turned back to look at his friend.

"What?" Bob said, perplexed. "What?"

Joe raised his eyebrows. "Nothing." He shrugged and turned around. "Nothing. What were you saying about the two actresses, Bob?"

"They're not the same. Two different actresses played the love interests of Dracula and the Mummy. The only connection between any of the movies so far is that the same actor who originated Frankenstein also originated the Mummy."

"But why did the mummy attack you?" Nina said. She steered the car toward the San Tomas Inlet Beach Walk. "Why does it want blood?"

"Maybe this Mummy needs blood to stay alive," Bob suggested.

"This still doesn't fit in with the movie," Nina said. "Nowhere in *The Mummy* does the creature go after someone's blood."

"Look," Joe said. "None of the monsters we've fought so far — Dracula, the Wolf Man, and Herr Frankenstein — have followed their scripts exactly. They've always added something a little extra. Dracula could turn into ticks; the Wolf Man took over a real person's body; and Herr Frankenstein knew more about DNA and computer programming than Steve Jobs and Bill Gates combined. Our Mummy has added his own little twist on his story."

"Levi said something interesting in Mrs. Hoving's class today about blood," Nina said. "All ancient people at some point in their cultural development have held the belief that the life force of a person could be found in several areas of the body. Some believed it was the flesh, some the liver, some the heart, some the intestines. Others believed that the blood of a person connected all these spiritual centers, and that by drinking the blood of an enemy or another person, the drinker would take on that person's strength and spirit."

"Is that what the Egyptians believed?" Bob asked.

"Yes," Nina replied. She looked at Bob in the rearview mirror.

Bob sat up and flashed back a small smile. Nina turned her eyes back to the road.

"Gonna be real interesting figuring out how to get the Mummy back into his movie on this one," Joe said after a moment of silence. "With each monster, it's more difficult. Dracula just went back into the camera without much of a fight."

"That's an understatement," Nina said.

"It would help if we could find the *Book of*

the Dead," Bob added. "I know it's just a book about Egyptian funerary rites and prayers, but the Mummy doesn't know that. Remember, he's dealing in two realities: the present reality into which he's been placed and the mythological reality of the movie. And in the movie, the *Book of the Dead* is a mystical book that contains the Scroll of Thoth and can bring someone back from death or send them to an early grave."

"Let's hope he doesn't know the difference between the two realities," Joe said.

"Here you go, madman," Nina said as she stopped behind the Beach Burger. "Remember, the exhibit opens at seven. Think you can get your mom to let you off work?"

"No problem. I'll just tell her that I need the extra credit to help my grade in English," Bob said as he hopped out of the car.

"Hey," Nina called after him. "You don't have to lie to your mom."

"Who's lying?" Bob said with a smile and a tip of his hat. "I'm off, said the madman," and he disappeared into the service entrance of the Beach Burger.

CHAPTER SIX

7 P.M., Convention Center
Opening of the Western Civilization Exhibit

"One thing we haven't really talked about," Joe was saying as he helped Nina finish sweeping up the mummy exhibit, "is who the Mummy is."

"Maybe it's Marvin. Angela says he's really creepy," Nina said, moving the broom across the floor quickly. She could hear Karl Homer speaking in the Greek exhibit room. He would soon have the VIPs in the Egyptian room, and she didn't want to be caught with a broom in her hands. "Remember, the Wolf Man was that nerdy deputy sheriff, Chad Barnes. Marvin could be his twin brother."

"That's too coincidental," Joe said. He knelt down with the dustpan and dust brush and quickly swept the dust and dirt into the dustpan. Footsteps came toward them. He looked at Nina. Nina motioned for him to get rid of the dust and dirt quickly. He looked around and quickly dumped it behind the curtain near the back of the room. Joe threw the dust brush and dustpan behind the table holding the jars just as Homer and the VIPs entered the room.

"And here is Professor Tovar's prized collection," Homer said. He walked across the room followed by a string of local dignitaries: the mayor, school superintendent, local business leaders, newspaper publisher, and others. "Professor Tovar found the queen's tomb more than fifty years ago, while digging in a remote site not far from the famed Valley of the Kings, where the tomb of King Tutankhamen was discovered. The discovery placed the professor's name in the annals of archaeology history. The queen's treasure was still intact and only a little less valuable than King Tut's. As you know, many of the Egyptian tombs were raided by bandits over the years, and the treasures with which the pharaohs and queens had been buried have been lost forever. But our queen still has all of her treasures." Homer's arm swept the room. The guests oohed and aahed at the trove: gold jewelry, elaborately carved and painted furniture, miniatures of the queen's slaves and servants, games, food that had long ago petrified, scrolls, and even a mummified cat. "The Egyptian dead went to their graves with everything they would need for life in the hereafter."

Homer moved to the queen's sarcophagus

and pushed the ornate wooden lid to the side. A golden glow shone forth as light from the room seeped into the coffin. The VIPs stepped forward and gazed with wonder at the golden resting place of the queen. Although the face mask appeared to be a single sheet of gold, Nina knew that it was actually made up of several dozen squares of gold hammered so gently and expertly that they appeared as one. Bright royal-blue paint outlined the queen's headdress and gold collar. Even her eyebrows and eyelashes were painted. The queen's chest was covered by a breastplate just as ornate as the face mask. In the center of the breastplate was a large rendering of a bug.

"What's that bug there for?" one man asked.

"That's no ordinary bug," Homer replied. "That's a scarab, one of the most sacred images in the Egyptian religious beliefs."

"Why?" another man asked. "It looks like an ordinary beetle to me."

"The scarab is a beetle," Homer replied. "A dung beetle. It represents the afterlife. The ancient Egyptians were acute observers of life, and they often interpreted their observations in a religious way. When the Egyptians observed the common beetle emerging from a pile of dung, they assumed the bug was being hatched from the dung, coming to life. This they interpreted as a resurrection, and that they, too, would be resurrected into an afterlife. If you're interested, you can purchase Professor Tovar's book on Egyptology at the reception desk."

"Where is Professor Tovar?" one woman asked.

"He was called back to the university on urgent business," Homer explained. "The professor was especially excited when he discovered the queen's tomb because it was the first time that a second tomb had been found buried under the first. And here is what Professor Tovar found in that second tomb."

Homer moved to a large canvas tarp at the other end of the room. He flung it back, revealing a sarcophagus. Unlike the queen's sarcophagus, this coffin was plain wood — no paint, no ornamentation, no attempt to make the box look attractive in any way.

"It's still a mystery as to why this sarcophagus was buried under the queen's," Homer said, running his hands over the smooth and ancient wood. "What is also fascinating is that the mummy inside has no face mask or breastplate, no signs of who he was. In fact, all the professor has been able to determine is that this mummy is a male and may have been a priest. Perhaps the priest to our young queen. A priest who couldn't go on living without his queen."

Homer smiled. "But that makes for a good novel or a good movie, ladies and gentleman."

Nina and Joe made eye contact across the room. Little did Karl Homer know that the story he had just told *had* been a movie. Now they had the link they needed. The spirit of Imhotep must have been drawn to this queen and her priest, so similar to himself and his princess.

"Professor Tovar is only interested in reality," Karl Homer continued. "He has spent the last fifty years poring over the ancient scrolls found with the queen, trying to determine who this poor soul was and why he was buried in such a fashion." Homer began pushing the lid of the coffin to the side. "You won't find him as lovely as our queen over there, but you might find him interesting nonetheless." Homer pushed the lid to the side just as the guests reached the edge of the coffin.

Several of the women and one of the men screamed. Homer's smile faded. Perplexed, he looked into the coffin and gasped. Nina and Joe joined the group and stared into the coffin.

Joe gave Nina a knowing look, and Nina nodded in turn.

Professor Angus Tovar's dead eyes stared up from the inside of the priest's coffin. A small trickle of dry blood had crusted down the left side of the professor's lips. His neck was bent almost at a right angle to his body.

Professor Tovar, the dead Professor Tovar, held a small scrap of ancient and soiled cloth in his hand. A cloth that an ancient Egyptian mummy would have wrapped around him.

CHAPTER SEVEN
Two Hours Later

A zipping sound echoed in the quiet room. All heads turned to watch as the coroner finished closing up the plastic body bag that held the remains of Professor Angus Tovar. Two paramedics lifted the body bag onto a stretcher.

Detective Turner and Joe stood together in one corner of the room. Joe looked over at Nina, who sat next to Levi on the floor. Levi's eyes were puffy and his cheeks were red. "What are you going to do now?" he asked Turner.

"We'll have to close down the exhibition," Turner said.

"Do you have to do that?" Homer said. He sniffed. His eyes held back tears.

"'Fraid so," Turner replied.

Homer looked at Turner. "Why?"

"Why what?" Levi said as he approached the group, Nina beside him.

"Detective Turner wants to close down the exhibit," Homer replied.

"No," Levi said, looking down at Turner.

"That's not up to you, son," Turner said.

"I'm not your son," Levi said, punctuating each word.

"This is now a crime scene," Turner explained. "We can't have people walking all over this place. We don't even know where your father was killed."

"This exhibit was the most important thing in his life," Levi protested.

"Finding his killer is the most important thing in my life now," Turner said calmly.

"You believe he was murdered?" Homer said.

Turner looked at the professor's assistant. "I don't think Professor Tovar climbed into that coffin, broke his own neck, and then put the lid back on."

"What's going on?" Bob asked as he approached the group.

"Professor Tovar's been killed. They found his body in the second coffin," Joe explained.

"What second coffin? I don't remember there being a second coffin in here," Bob said.

"It was under a tarp," Levi explained. "My father liked to surprise the VIPs at the exhibits."

"Seems the coffin was found under the tomb of the queen," Joe explained further.

"Oh," Bob said. Then he looked up at Joe and Nina, the significance of that dawning on him. "Oh!"

"You have no right to shut down the exhibit," Levi said, turning back to the detective.

"I have the right, and I'm shutting it down."

Levi took a step toward the detective. Instinctively, Joe stepped to Turner's side. Homer put a hand on Levi's chest.

"Please, gentlemen," Homer said. "This isn't the time or place to discuss this." He looked at Turner. "Do you have to shut the exhibit down completely? The professor spent months putting it together and years gathering all the artifacts not only in this room but in all the rooms. He wouldn't want it shut down on account of his death."

"My father spent his life studying the past, studying what the dead had left behind," Levi said. "It would be an insult to shut down the treasures he has left behind in this exhibit."

"How long will it take the police to go over the place?" Homer asked.

"I'm not sure," Turner said.

"A day? Two days?" Homer continued.

"Maybe. Maybe longer," Turner said.

"By Saturday?"

"Yeah. They should be done by Saturday," Turner said.

Homer faced Levi. "We can reopen on Saturday, Levi. We can dedicate the exhibit to your father's memory. We've got to let the forensic scientists do their jobs."

Levi's face softened. He nodded, fought back a tear, turned, and walked out of the room. Nina ran after him.

"Let's get out of here and let the lab boys get to work. I'll take you two home," Turner said.

"Oh, boy," Bob said. "Can I turn on the siren and lights?"

Joe punched Bob in the arm.

"Owwww!"

"Have a little respect," Joe warned his friend.

CHAPTER EIGHT

10:30 P.M.
Atlantic Motel and Seaside Cabins
Room 13

Despite the chill that wafted in from the cold Atlantic, Nina felt particularly warm sitting next to Levi in the lounge chairs outside his motel room. The sun had set hours earlier, but the midwinter night was clear and a silver sliver of moon hung in the sky. She pulled the blanket a little tighter around her.

"I like the cold," Levi suddenly said. They had sat for many minutes without talking. After arriving at the motel an hour earlier, Levi insisted that they sit outside in the lounge chairs. They had spoken only a few words and then neither spoke for a long time. Nina didn't mind the silence. Despite the circumstances, she enjoyed being in Levi's company. Ever since their first meeting, Nina had felt close to the young graduate assistant.

"Why?" Nina said.

"It helps me feel. I wouldn't want to live in Fargo, North Dakota, or Nome, Alaska, but

I like the cold wind on my skin. I feel alive, as funny as that sounds."

"It doesn't sound so funny," Nina said.

"My father always said I had strange ideas." Levi stared out across the black sea.

"You like the cold. I don't think that's so strange."

"I also like garlic on just about everything." He looked at Nina and smiled. "I mean everything."

"Still not strange," Nina replied. "Bob likes peanut butter and bologna sandwiches."

Levi sat silently for a few moments. Then he said, "Now, that's strange." He laughed, and Nina laughed with him. Then his smile dropped. "Guess I'll have to make funeral arrangements tomorrow. Probably have the funeral at the university."

"Can't your mother do that?"

"She's dead," he said without emotion.

"I'm sorry," Nina said softly.

"No. It's okay." He continued to stare out over the sea. "The faculty will probably want a big to-do. Dad would like something simple. Besides, I want to be back by Saturday. I've decided to rename the exhibit the Angus Tovar Exhibit in his honor."

"That's nice."

"He wouldn't like it. He didn't like taking credit for a lot of things, unlike some of his colleagues. Sometimes they would take credit for things he had discovered, and he'd let them. He'd tell me that the important thing was the find, not who got credit."

"That sounds like the noble act of a great man."

Levi smiled. "You've been watching too many old movies."

Nina frowned. "I'm being sincere."

"I'm sorry," Levi said. "I know you are." He swallowed. "I have to leave tomorrow, but I'll be back on Friday."

"Call me," Nina said. "You know, if you just want to talk."

Levi nodded.

A low growl sounded in the air around them.

"What?" Nina said.

"I didn't say anything."

The growl sounded again.

"Is that the ocean?" Levi said, sitting up.

"No," Nina replied. Both she and Levi stood. Nina stared into the black night. She could make out the gentle white froth from the black sea as it hit the black beach, a gentle splash hitting the sand.

The growl came again, louder and deeper this time.

Nina looked to her right.

Two sets of red eyes stared back at her. Goose

bumps crawled up her skin. She felt Levi grab her, hold her tighter.

The eyes moved forward into the yellow light just above the door to Levi's room.

"Oh, my God —" Nina began.

A tall, thin dog with a shiny black coat stood next to a small baboon. Both had red eyes that pierced the night like pinpoint lasers. Both had their black lips pulled back over black gums. Both had long, ugly, sharp-looking fangs with dark saliva dripping from them.

And both pounced on Nina and Levi as the couple screamed into the dark night.

CHAPTER NINE
Same Time

"If my mother and father find out I've snuck out of the house, I'm going to tell them that you hypnotized me and made me into your living zombie," Joe said as he tried to jimmy open a window at the back of the convention center.

"They won't believe you," Bob said as he held the small flashlight on his friend's hands.

"Why not?" Joe strained against the latch.

"Your parents don't think I'm that smart."

"That's true," Joe grunted.

"Sometimes it pays to play the fool."

"There!" Joe said with a groan. A metallic snap told him that the latch had given. He pushed and the window slid to the side. He hoisted himself up and through the opening. Bob handed him the small flashlight.

Bob jumped, grabbed the edge of the window, and tried to pull himself up. He strained and groaned and mumbled but could advance no farther than his chin on the windowsill's edge.

Joe poked his head out. "Hurry up, we don't have all night."

"You had to pick the window highest from the ground, didn't you?" Bob continued to struggle his way up, his toes trying to dig into the sides of the building.

"You picked the window, buddy."

"Yeah? Well, you didn't have to agree to it. You could have said, Hey, let's pick a window closer to the ground."

"Yeah, and I could have said, No, I'm staying in bed and not sneaking out of the house."

"You have all the answers, don't you?"

"At least I'm in the building."

Bob stopped struggling and looked at his large friend. "Well, don't just do something — stand there."

Joe laughed, reached down, and pulled his short friend through the window.

Bob bent over trying to catch his breath. "Middle of winter," he panted. "Cold wind — fifty-four degrees — and I'm sweating like a fat man in a sauna."

"You are a fat —"

"Hey!" Bob said.

"Don't open the can unless you plan on eating the worms."

"Gross. Where did you hear that one?"

"I just made it up."

"Yeah, well maybe Jay Leno could hire you. He hasn't been as funny as you lately. Let's go." Bob started off down the hallway.

They had entered through a window in the Renaissance exhibit and quickly made their way to the Egyptian room. They examined the coffin in which Professor Tovar had been found.

"It's got that same gray dust," Joe said. "Just like what was left on me."

"If I was a betting man, I'd say this is Imhotep's coffin," Bob said. "And the Mummy has risen."

"But there never was an Imhotep," Joe said. "It's only a story. Never was a high priest who tried to bring his loved one back to life. All of that was just fiction."

"Fiction or not, it's real enough now," Bob added. "Dracula wasn't real, either. Neither was the Wolf Man or Herr Frankenstein, but I'm still having nightmares from meeting them."

"I wonder whose coffin this was and why it was buried beneath the queen's? Can you read any of these hieroglyphics?"

Bob frowned at this friend. "I'm barely passing English, and you expect me to be able to read Egyptian hieroglyphics?"

"You can read FORTRAN like it's from a

first-grade reading book. And I've seen you decipher those cryptograms that Ms. Bashara hands out before she's done handing them out."

"I grew up reading FORTRAN, and the cryptograms that Ms. Bashara hands out are simple. This" — he pointed at the pictographs of men, baboons, birds, jackals, ankhs, wheat, and water — "is a language, not a code."

Joe shrugged. "Just thought I'd ask."

"Look at this," Bob said, holding up the mummified cat. "This looks like a mummified cat."

"It is a mummified cat," Joe said.

"What?" Bob replied, surprised, and dropped the ancient relic.

"Hey!" Joe shouted as he caught the cat before it hit the ground. "You're lucky that didn't break." He placed the cat back on the elaborately carved gold-leaf table.

"Who would want to mummify a cat?"

"The Egyptians took everything with them to the grave, including their pets, so they could have them to play with in the afterlife."

"If this is what they did to the things they loved, I'd hate to be something they hated."

"Yeah, they drank the blood of their enemies. Remember what Nina said."

"This isn't the time to remind me." Bob looked around the funerary table. "What are we looking for, anyway?"

"How should I know? You got me out of bed, remember?"

"Oh, yeah. I just want to check for any clues as to who might be the Mummy. I'm not so sure it's Marvin."

"I thought perhaps it was the professor until he turned up dead."

"Could be Levi."

"Could be."

"Maybe it's Homer."

"It could be anybody associated with the exhibits," Joe said in exasperation. "This isn't getting us anywhere. What are we looking for?"

Bob stopped. "Maybe we're looking for something that isn't here."

"What?"

"Maybe we're looking for a Maltese falcon."

"What are you talking about?" Joe shook his head. "You've been watching way too many of those old detective movies."

"In *The Maltese Falcon*, everyone is killing everyone else for this statue of a bird encrusted with expensive jewels, and then it turns out the bird probably doesn't even exist."

"Great," Joe said. "You just ruined that movie for me. I haven't seen it yet."

"Sorry. But, I'm making a point."

"Other than the one on the top of your head?"

Bob ignored his friend. "Look." He pointed

at two jars on the table. "Only two canopic jars. There's supposed to be four."

"A man, a baboon, a jackal, and a falcon," Joe said.

"And the jackal and baboon are missing."

"Were they here earlier?"

"I don't know," Bob said. "They're gone now."

"Wait a minute." Joe's eyebrows knitted together. "There were three of them earlier."

"How do you know?"

"Nina and I were cleaning up in here, and I saw them then. I remember now — there were only three. I didn't realize one was missing."

"Do you remember which ones were here?"

"The jackal, the falcon, and the man."

"So, the baboon was missing and now someone's stolen the jackal. Why? Morbid curiosity?"

"Then why not take all of them?"

"Maybe only time to take one. There were at least two dozen people in here when I arrived," Bob said. "Anybody could have taken it."

"It is valuable. But who would be cold enough to steal a priceless artifact from a dead man while his body was still in the room?" Joe asked, puzzled.

"The same person who would want the professor dead. These things are valuable, but only to museums. No one actually collects canopic jars. Each piece of the exhibit is numbered and registered." Bob held up one of the jars, holding the lid on so the dusty remains of entrails would not spill out. "See?"

"How did you know that?"

"Hannah told me when we were setting up one of the other exhibits."

"Then why would someone want to steal a canopic jar?"

"Each jar holds some part of the mummified person. The human-headed jar holds the liver; the baboon holds the lungs; the falcon holds the intestines; and the jackal holds the stomach. Each was preserved so the person would have them in the afterlife."

"You think the Mummy stole them?"

"He's going to need all the parts of his dead girlfriend if he's to bring her back to life, right?"

"Why not all the jars at once?"

"Maybe he's only taking what he can get away with."

Joe's eyes lit up. "Maybe the blood isn't just for him. Maybe he needs the blood for his girlfriend, too." The pair turned slowly. Joe pointed the flashlight at the gold face mask of the queen.

"I'd hate to see what she looks like after three thousand five hundred years," Bob said.

Joe looked at his watch. "Let's head home.

We'll tell Nina tomorrow, and we've got to tell Detective Turner, too."

Bob nodded and they began to work their way back to the Renaissance exhibit and the jimmied window. They walked quickly and in silence. Joe shuddered as they passed a replica of a rack, complete with a victim having his joints pulled out of their sockets.

"Ancient chiropractors," Bob quipped in a whisper.

"Not funny," Joe said. "There it is." He pointed to the small light at the open window. "I'm ready to get out of here. This place is creepy."

"Creepy is as creepy does," Bob said.

A slight wind scurried across the back of Bob's neck. He reached behind and rubbed his neck. He kept moving toward the window. The wind again brushed up against his neck.

Bugs! he thought. *I hate bugs!* He slapped the back of his neck.

"What?" Joe said, startled.

"Bugs."

"You hate bugs."

"I know," Bob said with a sneer.

Again, a slight wind moved across his neck. Bob turned around and stared straight into the oncoming blade of a medieval executioner's ax.

CHAPTER TEN
A Few Moments Later

"Levi!" Nina screamed as the baboon and dog leaped at them.

Levi picked up a lounge chair and threw it at the jackal. The metal chair hit the dog in the chops, and the beast yelped and fell to the ground.

The baboon was on Nina. Nina beat the beast about the face, trying to avoid the snapping of its sharp, wet teeth. The baboon screamed, its blue nose shining in the dim moonlight. Nina fell back onto the sidewalk. The baboon struck her about the face with a balled, leathery fist. Nina slapped at the baboon's snout. With each strike, the baboon bit at her hand. Hot, rancid spittle landed on her face.

Nina grabbed the baboon by the throat and began to squeeze the beast's neck. The baboon gagged for air and grabbed Nina's wrists. It squirmed to free itself from Nina's strong grip. It released Nina's wrist and began to hit her about the face again. The more it pounded, the harder Nina squeezed. After several moments, the baboon's blows lessened in intensity and in number. Nina saw the beast's eyes begin to roll back into its skull. The baboon went limp, and Nina threw the beast from atop her.

Nina crawled to her feet. "No!" she said in a hoarse whisper as she saw Levi lying prone a few feet from her, the dog hovering over his still body like a wild beast protecting its kill. Nina picked up her overturned lounge chair and moved toward the dog.

"Okay, Lassie," she said with a sneer. "Time to go find little Timmy." She swung the chair. The dog jumped back, snapping at the chair as it flew past. "Go on! Get! Go home! Bad dog! Bad dog!" With each command, she swung the chair, backing the dog away from Levi, off the sidewalk and into the soft sand. The dog stumbled as it hit the sand. It crouched, ready to leap.

A squeal erupted from behind Nina. She turned just in time to see the baboon leaping at her. She swung the chair, hitting the baboon across the jaw. The baboon screamed, hit the ground, rolled, and then darted off into the darkness of the beach. The dog snapped one last time at Nina and then followed the baboon into the darkness.

"Levi!" Nina said, her throat dry, her voice

cracking. She knelt next to Levi and turned him onto his back. "Levi?" she said softly.

Levi took a deep breath and slowly opened his eyes. He tried to speak, but the words were unintelligible.

"Levi," Nina said. She lifted his head and shoulders into her lap.

"I'm — okay — I — think," Levi finally managed.

"Are you bitten anywhere?"

"I don't think so." He sat up and rubbed the back of his neck. "I must have tripped or something, hit my head." Nina helped him to stand. "I don't understand what happened."

"We were attacked by a baboon and a dog."

"Jackal," Levi corrected.

"What?"

"That wasn't a dog, it was a jackal," Levi explained.

"You mean like in ancient Egypt?"

"Modern Egypt has them, too." Levi set the chairs upright and then sat in one. "What I don't understand is what a jackal would be doing in Florida." He turned to Nina. "Any zoos around here?"

"Only the high school."

"The high school has a zoo?"

"No," Nina said, shaking her head. "It was a lame attempt at humor."

Levi frowned. Then his face smoothed out. "Oh." He chuckled. "I get it. That's funny."

"I'm sorry. I shouldn't be joking on a night like this."

"It's a natural reaction," Levi said. He frowned again. "Why would a jackal and a baboon be together? The two are enemies."

"I don't know," Nina said, chewing her lip.

"I thought jackals had gray fur. This one was black," Levi pointed out.

"Like from an Egyptian painting," Nina said, her voice rising.

"Like an Egyptian painting from an Egyptian tomb," Levi added.

Nina thought for a moment, then asked Levi, "Do you ever watch old horror movies?"

CHAPTER ELEVEN
Back at the Convention Center

"Duck!" Joe yelled.

"I am! I am!" Bob yelled back as he bent down, the axman's blade swinging inches over his head. Bob scurried away from the axman as fast as he could.

Joe was hunched over, too, and the pair made their way through the displays. They heard the splintering of wood as the ax connected with the unlucky displays.

"You notice how he just keeps moving forward, swinging that ax at the same level?" Joe said, huffing.

"Yeah," Bob replied. "Like some sort of mad reaper."

The light from the tiny flashlight bounced in front of them as they ran. Joe did his best to light their way, to keep them from bumping into displays, but they knocked over mannequins, tables, chairs, benches, and just about everything else that stood between them and

the open window. The crashing and splintering of items behind them told them that the axman hadn't given up his pursuit.

"This definitely isn't in the movie!" Bob
yelled out.

"No time to argue movie trivia, Ebert," Joe
responded.

"Hey! You calling me fat?" Bob pushed his
friend, but Joe kept his balance.

"Can't this wait until later?" They neared
the window.

"You know how sensitive I am about my
weight!" Bob stood up.

"How sensitive are you about keeping your
head? Duck!" Joe grabbed his friend by the
neck and forced Bob to bend over. The blade
swished over the top of both of their heads.
"Let's just get out of here, and I'll write you an
apology in the paper, okay?"

They reached the window and both tried to
go through at the same time, squeezing themselves into the small opening.

"Well, this is another fine mess you've gotten
me into," Joe said, pushing on his shorter friend.

"Hey! Why are you pushing me back?" Bob
protested. "Why don't you push me forward?"

"Because the biggest part of you is behind
you," Joe blurted.

"You *do* think I'm fat and now you're saying
I've got a big butt!"

"I think your head is fatter than your butt, but we can argue anatomical semantics later." Joe gave a final push and Bob popped back into the room, landing on his rear.

Bob sat facing the slowly approaching ax-man, the silver blade glinting the little moonlight that streamed in through the window. Bob's eyes widened, and he tried to move. Fear held him in place. He felt his heart beating against his chest. The voice within his head screamed, *Move! Move! Move!* But Bob sat frozen on the wooden floor, the axman and his deadly blade inching toward him.

Bob suddenly felt two strong hands on his shoulders and then felt himself being lifted from the floor. In the blink of an eye, he was being dragged through the window. He hit the cold, wet ground with a thud, the air momentarily knocked out of him.

Bob and Joe lay panting on the ground, the night's dew soaking into their jackets. They listened between breaths to the splintering of wood as the axman continued destroying the exhibit.

"Let's go," Joe said. He rolled over, stood, and started to trot away from the convention center.

"Hey! Not so fast," Bob said. "Slow down, will ya?"

"I'm not slowing down until I'm home and under the covers! This was a great idea you had!"

"Yeah? Well, hindsight is always twenty-twenty."

"If that's true," Joe retorted, "then you ought to put glasses on your butt and walk through life backward!"

Even Bob couldn't come up with a good comeback to that one.

CHAPTER TWELVE
Tuesday
Nina's Home
7:30 A.M.

Nina sat at her kitchen table, eating soggy cereal and trying to wake herself up. She hadn't slept much that night. She had confided in Levi about the 3-D projector and how she, Joe, and Bob had released the six monsters from their movies. She told him how they had defeated Dracula, the Wolf Man, and Frankenstein, and how now they all believed they were fighting the Mummy. She told him about the mummy and the man in the fez who had attacked Joe. Levi became angry and told her that he was a scientist, that he didn't believe in fairy tales, that the movies weren't real, and that he didn't have time to listen to any more of Nina's stories.

He had stormed into his room and had begun throwing clothes into a sports bag, explaining that it was late and he had to make his father's funeral arrangements. The last words he uttered as he pushed the clothes into the bag kept her from sleeping most of the night:

I don't have time to play games with little high-school girls!

Nina fought back a tear. She stacked the plates, rose from the table, and placed them in the kitchen sink. Perhaps it was for the best. He was six years older than she, a graduate assistant who had been around the world and had visited exotic places, while she was just a girl who was born and raised in San Tomas Inlet, which was about as exotic as cold macaroni.

Nina was numb for the rest of the day, going through the motions of paying attention in class, dutifully handing in her homework, making her way through the crowded hallways, and hoping that she would curl into a little ball and just blow away. The first boy she'd ever liked had called her a little high-school girl.

"Hey, Zombie Head!" a distant voice yelled, breaking through her self-pity party. "Zombie Head!"

Nina blinked. Her eyes focused on Captain Bob. *From bad to worse*, she thought.

"Hey," Bob repeated as he and Joe approached her. "We've been looking for you all day. You weren't in the cafeteria at lunch and we didn't see you in the hallways between classes."

"I don't want to burst your bubble, Bob, but it may come as some surprise to you that my day isn't planned around the times I might see you. I have other things and other people in my life, you know."

"You mean like Mr. Graduate Assistant?" Bob said, and then he regretted the harshness in his voice. "Sorry. I didn't mean that the way it sounded."

"Yes, you did," Nina said. "But I think that's what I like about you, Captain Bob: You're honest without knowing it, and you live in the moment."

Bob looked at Joe. "Is that good? What she said?"

"It's good," Joe replied. "We have something to tell you about the exhibits."

"Walk and talk, gentlemen," Nina said as she headed to the exit leading to the school parking lot. "Because I have something to tell you as well." They piled into Nina's Camaro and headed toward the Beach Burger.

"I'll be glad when the Atomic Drive-in is re-opened," Bob said. "I'm tired of eating my own cooking."

"Two more weeks," Joe said. Bob smiled, and then Joe related the story of the attack of the medieval axman. He was still perplexed as to the man's mechanical movements. Then he told her about the missing canopic jars in the Egyptian exhibit.

"Which jars?" Nina said, her eyes focused on the road.

"The monkey and the dog," Bob chimed in.

"Baboon and jackal," Joe corrected.

"You boys are going to like this, then," Nina said. "Levi and I were attacked by a baboon and a jackal last night at his motel room."

"You went to his motel room?" Bob said, astonished.

"Are you sure?" Joe said.

"Yes," Nina replied.

"Why did you go to his motel room?" Bob said.

"What happened?" Joe said.

"The baboon attacked me," Nina replied.

"He attacked you?" Bob said incredulously. "I knew that creep was a creep!"

Joe spun around in his seat. "What are you talking about?"

"That creep. Mr. Graduate Assistant. Mr. I-Know-Everything-About-Ancient-Egypt! That's what I'm talking about."

"I don't know what you're talking about," Joe said, confused.

"That creep attacked Nina at his motel room!" Bob shouted.

Joe frowned. "Why do I feel like I'm in a

Tim Burton movie when I'm around you? Levi didn't attack Nina. A baboon attacked Nina. A real baboon."

Bob sat back, his face suddenly blank. "Oh. Oh, that's different. That's okay, then."

"That's not *okay*!" Nina said. "The baboon was trying to kill me and the jackal went after Levi. I almost choked the baboon to death. And then I had to fight the jackal off of Levi."

"You had to fight the jackal off Levi?" Bob said, sitting forward. "What happened to Mr. Wonderful?"

"I don't know," Nina said through her teeth. "By the time I got the baboon off of me, Levi was unconscious and the jackal was about to attack him. Levi doesn't remember what happened to him."

"The jackal and the baboon canopic jars are missing, and you and Levi are attacked by a jackal and a baboon," Joe said thoughtfully. "This may sound crazy, boys and girls, but I think whoever Imhotep is, he's brought the canopic jars to life and is using them to kill anybody who knows their secret."

"You think that's what happened to Professor Tovar?" Bob said.

"His neck was broken," Joe replied. "Baboons are very strong, and the professor wasn't in the greatest shape. Wouldn't be hard for a baboon to break his neck."

They pulled into the Beach Burger parking lot and walked around to the front door.

"Garçon!" Bob said as they entered the popular fast-food restaurant.

"Hey, Captain Bob, my homey," Trey said from behind the counter.

"Where's Hubert?" Bob said as the trio slid into a booth.

"He said he had to run an errand and he'd be right back."

"He left you alone?" Bob said.

"No," Trey replied, looking around. "There are customers here. I'm sorry I couldn't work at the exhibit last night, but Tia Maria insisted I do my homework. Here." He handed a paper to Bob. Bob looked at the paper and frowned at Trey. "Tia Maria also says you have to do your own homework, homeboy."

"You're having Trey do your homework for you?" Nina asked.

"No," Bob replied in protest. "I just wanted him to show me how to do a few algebra problems so I could work out the rest for myself."

Nina grabbed the paper and scanned it quickly. "A few problems. You mean like numbers one through thirty-six?"

"Busted," Trey said, smiling.

Bob grabbed the paper back. "Okay, okay. I'll do it myself." Bob looked at Trey. "But I'm not helping you with your English anymore."

"Good," Trey said, wiping his brow in mock relief. "Maybe now I can learn the language properly."

"Fifty thousand comedians out of work, I get Cuba's answer to Chris Rock," Bob said with a grimace.

"What time do you have to be at the exhibit tonight?" Trey asked the group.

"No time," Bob said, and Trey frowned.

"It's closed until Saturday," Joe replied. "Professor Tovar was found murdered in the Egyptian room."

The smile fell from Trey's face. "Do you think it's the Mummy?"

"Looks that way," Nina said.

"Blood and thunder," Trey said. "That gives me the shaky shivers."

Nina frowned at Bob. "You *have* been teaching him English, haven't you?"

"Guilty," Bob replied with a smile.

Nina looked at Trey. "Trey, forget everything that Bob has taught you."

"Why?" Trey asked ingenuously.

"Because Bob's vocabulary is better suited for the 1930s than the twenty-first century."

"Willikers," Bob replied in a faux Southern accent. "I have been lampooned by the fairer sex."

"I'm gonna lampoon you like a beached

whale if you make another sexist remark like that!" Nina fired in return.

"Are you saying I'm fat?" Bob cried.

"Here we go again," Joe said with a grimace. "Trey, bring me a large diet cola and a large bottle of aspirin to wash it down with."

"Righty-o, guv'nor," Trey said in a terrible British accent. He trotted away.

"There you three are," Detective Turner said as he walked up to the table. "I just came from the school but you had apparently left."

"Apparently," Bob said.

Turner sat next to Nina. "I'm glad to see you're your surly self today," he said to Bob. Bob shrugged. "I just came from the convention center and —"

"And the place looked like a mad axman had chopped the place up," Bob finished.

Turner sat back. "How did you know that?"

"Because a mad axman did chop it up," Joe said. "We were there last night, and he was trying to kill us."

Turner laughed.

"What's so funny?" Bob said with a frown.

"He wasn't trying to kill you."

"You think he was just looking for firewood?" Bob said.

"He wasn't looking for anything," Turner replied. "He was a robot. Professor Tovar had gotten it from one of those pizza places that used to have robots. He dressed it like a medieval executioner to demonstrate how the executioner would do his job. Now that I know you two were there, I also know how he accidentally got turned on." Turner eyed Bob.

"I didn't touch nothing," Bob protested.

"Anything," Nina corrected. "You didn't touch anything."

"You weren't even there," Bob said with a frown.

"That explains why he moved so slowly and seemed to be only chopping one way," Joe said.

"Just what were you two doing there?" Turner said.

Joe explained about the canopic jars and then Nina explained about the attack on her and Levi. Turner listened with interest and then sat back in the booth.

"First of all, this better be the last time you guys do a B&E," Turner finally said.

"What's a B&E?" Bob whispered to Nina.

"Breaking and entering, you idiot," Nina replied.

"You caused some serious damage, and if I have to cover for you one more time, my ass is on the line," Turner continued. "Now, want to know how the professor died?"

"Broken neck, wasn't it?" Bob said.

"Yes, but that's not the strange part," Turner said. "Forensics came back with an interesting set of prints around the professor's neck. Prints with thin palms and long thin fingers. They made a cast of the imprint. And guess what."

"They're not human," Nina said.

"They're baboon," Joe added.

"That's just peachy," Bob said.

Nina frowned. "We also believe that Imhotep, whoever he is, has turned the canopic jars into living beings and that he needs blood to stay alive. The ancient Egyptians believed that drinking blood empowered them with the spirits of their foes and helped keep them immortal."

"They predate Dracula," Turner said.

"Not the same thing," Bob said. "Dracula drank the blood of the good and the evil. The ancient Egyptians only drank the blood of their enemies. They weren't bloodthirsty. In a way, they were honoring their enemies."

"Still gives me the heebie-jeebies," Turner said.

"If Imhotep is turning the jars into living beings, that means that he'll go after the human-headed and the falcon-headed jars next," Joe said.

"That's logical," Nina said.

"But why?" Bob said. "Why does he need them? In the movie, he discovered that the spirit of his long-lost princess was reincarnated in the body of Helen Grosvenor, and he had to read from the Scroll of Thoth in order to bring his lost love back to life. Why does he need all the canopic jars to come to life?"

"They represent the gods," Nina said. "In the movie, Imhotep failed in his attempt to bring his beloved Princess Anck-Su-Namun back to life because he lacked the power. He was finally transformed from Ardeth Bey back into the Mummy, where he disintegrated into thirty-five-hundred-year-old dust."

"So now, having learned from his mistakes he's lining up as many ancient Egyptian gods as he can to help him raise his Anck-Su-Namun back to life," Bob concluded. "Somehow Professor Tovar found out and Imhotep fitted him with a wooden overcoat."

"What?" Turner said.

"He's into old gangster movies now," Joe explained.

"That still doesn't tell us who Imhotep is," Nina said.

"Karl Homer is my candidate," Joe said. "He was the last person to see Professor Tovar alive, and he claimed to have received a telegram from the professor at our first meeting. And now we know that Tovar didn't go back to the university and that the telegram was a fake."

"I've seen the telegram," Turner said. "And it's not fake. It was sent from the Western Union branch office at the university the night the professor was killed. Another strange thing about all this: The coroner put the professor's death at about midnight. The telegram, supposedly sent by the professor, was time-stamped at eight o'clock that evening, four hours before the professor's death."

"Then who sent the telegram?" Bob said.

"I called Western Union's branch office at the university. The clerk remembered a tall man, rather old, wearing a funny hat and claiming to be the professor. The man knew it wouldn't be delivered until the next day."

"Funny hat?" Nina said.

"Yeah, the guy said it was round and tapered toward the top, which was flat."

"A fez," Joe said.

"Yep," Turner replied. "I've calculated the travel time from the university to the convention center."

"Four hours, right?" Bob chimed in.

"Three and a half hours," Turner corrected. "Enough time to allow our Imhotep to send the telegram from the university, travel back to San Tomas, and kill the professor."

"But why?" Joe asked.

"Maybe because he knew about the Scroll of

Thoth," Nina said. The others looked at her. "It's hidden in the Ptah-Soker-Osiris."

Joe whistled. "That's the scroll in the movie that Imhotep uses to bring Anck-Su-Namun back to life."

"You know," Bob said thoughtfully, "Imhotep really does fail in the movie. The spirit of Anck-Su-Namun is awakened in Helen Grosvenor, but it is Helen Grosvenor's love for Frank Whemple that keeps her from fully succumbing to the Mummy's lure. When Imhotep realizes his long-lost love has finally rejected him, he has nothing to live for, literally."

"That's sad," Nina said distantly.

"That still leaves us with only Karl Homer as Imhotep," Turner said. "Any other suspects? You kids are better at this celluloid guessing game than I am."

"Marvin," Joe said. "Any of the other graduate assistants."

"How about Hannah Tucker?" Bob said. The others frowned at him. "Why not? A short, pigtailed, know-it-all girl with the personality of a slug. It's the perfect disguise for a bloodthirsty monster."

"I don't think so," Joe said. "So far the monsters have taken on the guises of a dentist, a deputy sheriff, and a high-school biology teacher, but they were all of the right gender. Imhotep is a male; therefore, his disguise will be a male, also."

"Then there's Levi Tovar," Turner said absentmindedly.

"What?" Nina said, looking up.

"Levi Tovar," Turner repeated. "He could be Imhotep."

"Yeah, and I'm Helen Grosvenor," Nina said with a nervous laugh.

"Hey, if my favorite teacher could turn out to be a mad scientist," Bob chimed in, "I don't see why your boyfriend can't turn out to be a long-dead, dried-up old mummy."

Nina frowned. Then she smiled. "We were both attacked by the baboon and the jackal last night. If he were Imhotep, they wouldn't have attacked him."

"Maybe he's just trying to make himself look innocent," Bob said, shrugging.

"Okay," Turner said. "Let's just keep our eyes on everybody associated with the exhibit. Everyone's a suspect until one of us can say for certain who the real Imhotep is."

"Here's your diet cola," Trey said as he walked up to the booth. He set the glass in front of Joe. "I couldn't find a bottle of aspirin, but I did find some Tic Tacs for you."

"At least your breath will have that minty-fresh feeling," Bob said.

"I can still smell the peanut butter and bologna on *your* breath, Bob," Nina said, waving her hand in front of her nose.

"Well," Bob replied, grinning. "Then don't inhale."

CHAPTER THIRTEEN
Convention Center
6:30 P.M.

"I told you, they're not pigtails." Hannah Tucker glowered at Bob.

"I wish you would stop teasing her about her hair," Joe said. "It's getting annoying."

"Well, they look like pigtails," Bob said with mock innocence.

"Ponytails!" Hannah insisted.

"Okay, okay," Bob said, his face grimacing. "Man, is this what it's like to have a little sister?"

"When you two are done cleaning up in here, Mr. Homer said you're to check the Age of Exploration and make sure that all the explorers are properly set and with the right charts." Hannah turned and stomped out of the Renaissance exhibit.

"How did so much bossiness get put into so little a person?" Bob said, making sure that Hannah was out of hearing range.

"I don't know, but if you make fun of her pigtails, I mean ponytails, one more time, I'm going to put *your* head in pigtails."

Bob rubbed the stubble on top of his head. His hair was slowly but surely growing out. Bob thought he looked tough with his burr hairstyle, but Nina said he looked like a cue ball with fungus. He had still failed to think of a good reply to that little quip, but he would.

Joe scooped up a small pile of wooden splinters and dumped them into a trash can. "You finish up in here," he said to Bob. "I want to check something in the Egyptian room. I'll meet you in the Age of Exploration."

"Okay," Bob said without protest.

Joe shrugged and made his way through the exhibits. He wanted to search the room before Hannah the Horrible, as Bob now called her, discovered he was missing from his post.

The room was dead quiet as Joe entered. Joe shuddered. Twenty-four hours earlier, the body of Professor Tovar had been discovered in Imhotep's sarcophagus. Two of the canopic jars were missing and had been turned into living beasts, or at least that was their theory. And somewhere in San Tomas Inlet, the Mummy was stalking its next prey.

Joe walked over to the queen's coffin. The lid was still pulled back, revealing the golden mask and breastplate. Joe gently ran his fingers over the smooth metal. It was so old, and yet an energy seemed to surge from the gold-plated face of the long-dead queen.

He looked over the table holding the queen's prized possessions — possessions prized in life and in death: a comb; games; the mummified cat; jewelry; small models of a boat, a house, and servants; even a small tablet of clay upon which several letters of Egyptian demotic writing were inscribed.

Then Joe noticed the other two canopic jars were missing, the jars of Imset, the man, and Qebhesnuef, the falcon: the jars containing the liver and the intestines. Now Imhotep had them all: stomach, lungs, liver, and intestines. He had all the gods on his side. All he needed was to find the young woman who would be carrying the soul of his long-lost love.

Joe set to work quickly. He had come to the room expecting the other two jars to be missing; what he wanted to find were the wooden figurines of Ptah-Soker-Osiris. If Imhotep found them first, they would be powerless against the ancient priest. Joe looked through baskets and inside the wardrobe chest of the queen. He knew that the Ptah-Soker-Osiris could be large or small and were sometimes hidden in secret compartments of chests and boxes or even disguised as game pieces. The size of the Ptah-Soker-Osiris didn't matter; it was what was inside that made the wooden figurines important. The Scroll of Thoth was one of the most important items that Imhotep needed to cross over into the realm of the dead, the Egyptian equivalent of heaven.

Joe had searched the room and failed to find the figurines. There would be four. He had found some secret compartments in a few chests and boxes, but those were empty. He looked at his watch and then around the room one last time. He was about to leave to rejoin Bob and Hannah the Horrible when the leg of the queen's couch caught his eye. He had seen pictures of the couch from King Tut's tomb. A long couch shaped like a leopard with a thin seat and thin legs. The queen's couch was also shaped and painted like a leopard. The seat was long and thin, just like King Tut's. The difference was the legs. The legs of the queen's couch were thick, at least six inches thick, much thicker than the legs on King Tut's couch.

Joe crossed the room and knelt down. He tapped one of the legs. The knocking echoed within the wooden leg. If the leg had been solid, the sound would have been more of a thump. But the knock had echoed, as though it was bouncing off something inside the leg.

Joe lifted up the end of the couch and stared at the leg's bottom. It had been hollowed out to make room for something.

Joe tried to pry out the object, but it was so firmly wedged in that Joe surmised the only way to get it out was to break off the leg.

Joe looked the leg over carefully. The builder of the couch wouldn't have just shoved the object up into the hollowed-out leg. The Egyptians were too clever and loved puzzles too much to do something so crude. Joe ran his fingers along the edge of the leg until he felt a slight indentation. He pressed the indentation and heard a wooden snap. The object slid out of the leg ever so slightly, revealing a painted base with feet. Joe pulled the object all the way out from the leg. It was a Ptah-Soker-Osiris, painted to look like one of the gods, perhaps Isis or Osiris himself or even Ra, the sun god. Whichever god was presented on the wooden figurine, Joe knew that he now held in his hand one-fourth of the secret chants and prayers that were written especially for the young queen who lay in her gilded coffin a few feet away.

Joe opened the base of the wooden statue and pulled out a papyrus scroll. He gently unfurled the scroll; the ancient papyrus cracked and resisted. Joe squinted to see between the edges of the scroll. The dyes used to paint the hieroglyphics of the prayers and chants were still brilliant with color. Joe didn't know what words or magic spells the pictographs formed, but he knew that they could be used to bring the young queen back to life. The scrolls contained within all four legs of the couch were the Scroll of Thoth, the ancient and forbidden scroll that could resurrect the dead.

Joe quickly retrieved the remaining three scrolls from the couch's legs. He was turning to leave when he found himself standing face-to-face with an Egyptian warrior. At first, Joe thought perhaps it was just a mannequin he had failed to notice when he entered the room. So he stepped to the side. The Egyptian warrior mirrored his move.

The warrior was dressed in a shiny brass breastplate carved with the falcon head, the god Horus, god of war. His brass shield had a golden sheen. His helmet was as bright as the breastplate, and the sword that hung at his side gleamed a white silver. The warrior's left arm was held at a right angle to his body. A falcon sat at the crook of the warrior's elbow.

Joe made a move back to his left. The warrior followed suit. The falcon leaned forward, adjusting his stance on the warrior's arm, the razor-sharp talons digging into the leather band covering the warrior's skin. Its mouth opened slightly, the hooked beak revealing the needle-point edge.

Joe thought perhaps he could get past the

warrior, but he couldn't outrun the falcon. He held up the four scrolls.

"You want these?" Joe said, understanding that the warrior could no more understand modern English than Joe could understand ancient Egyptian. There was something comforting in hearing his own voice, Joe thought. At least if he could hear his voice, he knew he was still alive. "You want these?" Joe repeated.

Joe thrust the scrolls to the right. The eyes of the man and the falcon followed. He thrust them to the left. The eyes of the two ancients followed to the left. Joe held them up, and their heads turned upward. Then Joe thrust the scrolls downward.

When the warrior and the falcon turned their heads down, Joe grabbed the tarp that was still partially draped over Imhotep's coffin and tossed it over the Egyptian warrior and the falcon. The falcon cried out as it tried to fly away before it was trapped under the tarp.

Joe bolted from the room, through the ancient Greek room and into the Roman Conquest room. He heard the cry of a bird behind him. Just as he was heading into the Rise of the Celtic Tribes, Joe felt a sharp sting on the back of his head and then felt something hard and heavy strike him in the head. He sprawled to the floor, maintaining his grasp on the papyrus scrolls. He reached behind and touched the back of his head with his free hand. A fire of pain shot throughout his skull. Blood stained his fingers.

He glanced up to see the falcon sitting on the ax blade of a ferocious-looking redheaded Celtic warrior, whose battle-ax was raised high over his head, with a look of eternal hatred on his face.

Joe pushed himself up as a layer of darkness slowly descended upon him. The falcon leaned forward, ready to swoop down and strike Joe again.

"You want these?" Joe said slowly, barely understanding his own words. He moved the scrolls back and forth, and the falcon followed the movement.

From behind him, Joe heard a clank of metal. He turned slowly. The Egyptian warrior glared at Joe. The blanket of darkness slowly pulled itself up to Joe's chin — warm and secure.

"You — want — these?" Joe heard the words but didn't recognize his own voice.

The ancient Egyptian warrior raised his gleaming silver sword over his head. Joe watched as the weapon of death descended toward his own head.

CHAPTER FOURTEEN

"Hey, Joe!" Bob said with a chuckle as he entered the Rise of the Celtic Tribes room. "If Hannah the Horrible catches you sleeping on the job, she'll —"

The falcon screamed. Bob turned toward the noise just as the bird of prey launched itself from the ax of the Celtic warrior and dove for him, the razor-sharp talons aimed at his face.

"Yeow!" Bob shrieked. He was carrying several folded costumes in his arms. At the sight of the approaching bird of prey and its deadly talons, Bob tossed the costumes into the air. The falcon screamed as it dove into the layers of clothing, its talons hooking into the material. Bob ducked as the descending ball of bird and clothing whizzed past his head and slammed into the side of a Celtic tent.

"Joe!" Bob yelled when he saw the sword of the Egyptian warrior swing down at his best friend. Bob bolted toward the ancient warrior, ducking his right shoulder and slamming into the Egyptian's left side before the blade could finish its arc. Bob and the Egyptian slammed into a wooden loom. The loom exploded under the weight into a hail of wooden shards and splinters. Bob and the Egyptian crashed to the floor. The Egyptian lay still.

Bob jumped to his feet and dashed to Joe. "Joe," Bob said, his breathing hard and sharp. "Joe, are you all right?" Bob started to turn his friend over but stopped when he saw the thick, red goo at the back of Joe's head. "Joe," Bob said in a frightened whisper.

But then he spun around again. The Egyptian had recovered and was coming toward him, his sword pulled back, ready to bite the first bit of flesh its finely honed edge could kiss.

Bob screamed as the warrior swung the blade toward Bob's neck. Bob ducked as quickly as he could. The blade glided over his shirt and cut off two buttons. Then a sudden movement caught his eye. It was Hannah. She was standing at the door, near frozen with terror at the spectacle before her.

The Egyptian raised his sword over his head, aiming this time to split Bob in two.

Bob wasn't about to wait around and let that happen. He rolled to his left and jumped to his feet. "Hannah! Get help!" he commanded.

Hannah didn't move. Her face was ashen, and her eyes were bulging from their sockets.

"Hannah!" Bob yelled again. The little girl couldn't move. "Hey, pigtails!"

That got her attention. "They're not pig —"

The sword of the ancient Egyptian sailed inches from Bob's head. Hannah began screaming.

"Run, you little twerp!" he ordered. "Go get help!"

She ran.

Bob turned his attention back to the Egyptian warrior. At least he was between the ancient warrior and Joe, who was still lying motionless on the floor.

Bob picked up a splintered leg of the wooden loom. "All right, you piece of petrified history." He held the leg back, ready to swing.

The Egyptian raised his free left arm at a right angle to his body. The falcon swooped down from the corner and landed on the leather pad covering the Egyptian's arm. The deadly bird kept its keen eyes focused on Bob. The Egyptian mumbled.

"Huh?" Bob said instinctively. He squinted. Behind the Egyptian, silhouetted in the door, was a tall, thin man wearing a fez. The man was muttering something.

The Egyptian mumbled in reply, the words unintelligible, but deep and guttural. The dark man in the fez spoke again, his voice as deep and guttural as the warrior's. Abruptly, the Egyptian, with the falcon still delicately balanced on his arm, turned and left the room.

"Huh?" Bob said, surprised. He watched as all three disappeared into the darkness of the corridor. He was tempted to run after them, but stopped himself when he heard a groan behind him. Bob spun around. "What are you doing?" he blurted when he saw Nina and Stacy kneeling next to Joe.

"We just got here," Nina explained. "Hannah was in hysterics. We couldn't understand a word she was saying."

"She's still crying," Stacy said. "What happened in here? Who was that guy? Is he one of the grad assistants?"

"Joe," Nina said softly.

Joe stirred and rolled himself over. The back of his head hit the floor. "Oww!" he cried, grimacing. He lifted his head from the floor, some of the thick drying blood sticking to the floor.

"We've got to get him to the hospital," Nina said. She took out her cell phone and dialed 911.

"What was that, Bob?" Stacy said again.

"You saw them?" Bob said.

"Yeah, just as we came into the room," Stacy explained.

"Did you hear what he was saying?"

"No, he just looked at us, mumbled something, and left. Who *was* he?"

"King Tut," Bob said.

"Who?"

"Never mind."

"They're on their way," Nina said, turning off her phone. Joe tried to sit up, but Nina kept him from rising. "You stay still, big guy. Help is on the way. Turn to the side so the back of your head isn't against the floor."

Joe did as he was told.

"Gross," Stacy said with a grimace. "That's going to leave a scar."

"Why don't you make yourself useful and go get some towels?" Nina said, disgust in her voice.

"Yeah, like I know first aid or something," Stacy retorted.

"Just go get some towels!"

"The magic word would be helpful."

"Go get some towels, and I won't KILL you. Is that word magic enough for you?"

Stacy rolled her eyes. "Everything's a tragedy with you, isn't it?" She stood and strode out of the room before Nina could reply.

"What that girl needs is a knuckle sandwich," Nina said through gritted teeth.

"You been watching the same old gangster movies that Bob has?" Joe said, trying to put a lilt in his voice.

"If you're still able to crack jokes, then you'll be all right," Nina said with a smile.

"Here," Joe said. "These are what he and the bird were after." He held up the four scrolls to Nina.

"What are these?" Nina said, curious.

"The Scroll of Thoth," Bob answered.

"Right," Joe said, smiling at his friend.

"You found them," Nina breathed.

"The other two canopic jars —" Joe started.

"Just left the room," Bob finished. "I'd like to know when Imhotep had time to change the jars into the warrior and the falcon."

"I'd like to know who Imhotep is," Nina said. "We could bring this business to a close real fast."

"How?" Bob said pointedly. "You said yourself you didn't think the camera would even work on the Mummy, and a computer program isn't going to work on an ancient Egyptian like it did on Herr Frankenstein. Just how do you propose to send the Mummy back into his movie?"

Nina's eyes narrowed. "I'm going to let you breathe your peanut butter and bologna breath on him — he'll be begging to leave this reality."

CHAPTER FIFTEEN
Thursday, Two Days Later
5:30 P.M.
Beach Burger

"Your mom told me to tell you that you're to close tonight," Hubert said as he placed a tray of soft drinks on the table. Detective Turner, Joe, Nina, Angela, and Captain Bob had assembled to discuss their next step.

"You didn't get her note?" Bob said innocently as he passed the drinks around.

"What note?"

"Oh, I must have thrown it away." Bob rubbed his chin as if trying to remember what the nonexistent note said. "Let's see: 'Dearest Bob — I told Hubert you were to close tonight, but then I remembered that you have homework to do. Please ask Hubert nicely if he could close so you can do your homework. Love, Your Mother.' Yeah, that's what the note said." Bob put the straw in his mouth and slurped up a swig of diet cola. He looked at Hubert. "Hubert, could you please close up tonight so I can do my homework?" He batted his eyes at the young waiter.

"That's a bunch of hooey," Hubert said.

"Hubert, would I lie to you?" Bob asked innocently. "Call Mom. See if I'm lying."

"I'll do that," Hubert snorted as he stormed away.

"She'll tell him you're lying," Nina said.

"She's not home. It's bingo night — ladies half price. Mom never misses it." Bob had a look of triumph on his face.

"I see you either as a future infomercial salesman or a politician," Turner said, sipping his drink.

"Probably try to sell the country if he ever became president," Joe chimed in.

"How're the stitches?" Bob asked his friend.

"They don't hurt," Joe answered.

"Anybody have any concrete ideas about who Imhotep is?" Turner said, getting down to business.

"It's not Levi," Nina answered quickly. "He was in Miami at the university. The canopic jars of the man and the falcon were intact when he left."

"Marvin?" Turner said, looking at Angela.

"I'm staying away from that lovelorn geek," Angela said quickly. She swirled her straw in her soft drink. "Could be Marvin. He's quite knowledgeable about ancient history, especially Egypt."

"What about Egyptian funerary rites?" Nina said.

"I didn't stick around long enough to find that out. I asked Mr. Homer to switch me and he put Stacy in with him."

"Too bad," Nina said with a frown.

"For Stacy," Angela said with a chuckle.

"You didn't get a good look at the man in the corridor who spoke to the warrior?" Turner said.

"No, but the fez looked familiar," Bob said with a grin.

Nina rolled her eyes. "Don't you ever stop?"

"The man in the fez must be Imhotep," Joe said.

"I agree," Nina said.

"You're just agreeing because that would rule out Mr. Graduate Assistant," Bob blurted.

"I guess that it does," Nina said, cocking one eyebrow.

"Does what?" Levi said as he walked up to the table, a box in his hands.

"I thought you weren't coming back until tomorrow," Nina exclaimed.

"We had the memorial service this morning," Levi explained. "I took care of some business and then drove up here. No sense in waiting around when there's work to be done."

"What about the funeral?" Nina said.

"Dad didn't want a funeral. He was cremated." He held up the box.

Nina swallowed. She pointed at the box. "Is that —"

"Dad," Levi announced, holding up the box.

"Wow," Angela said softly.

"Cool," Bob said, then added, "Can I see the ashes?"

"Don't be so crude, Bob," Nina chided. She looked at Levi. "Why did you bring him here?"

"His will asked that he be placed with the exhibit," Levi said. "I thought I'd put him in one of the empty urns in the Egyptian display. That was his favorite." Levi looked at Turner. "We're still opening on Saturday, right?"

Turner sipped his drink, looked at the box, frowned, and said, "Yeah. We're done."

"Find anything?"

"It's better not to reveal what we found in the investigation," Turner said, businesslike. "The criminal knows certain things, and if we tip our hand that we know them, too, he might flee."

"Any suspects?"

"Everyone's a suspect until the real criminal is caught." Turner looked at this watch. "I've got a date with leftover meat loaf and a lounge chair," he said, rising. "They're rerunning last year's Daytona, and I don't want to miss it."

He threw his coat on and looked at Joe and Bob. "Keep in touch."

Bob watched as Turner left and then said, "Now that's sad. A young man like that, and he goes home to leftover meat loaf, a tattered lounge chair, and a rerun of a race he already knows the winner of. Could there be a more pathetic sight?"

"Yes," Nina said, smiling significantly at Bob.

The Convention Center
6:30 P.M.
American Inventors Exhibit

"I don't think it's very historically accurate to put Samuel Morse with Alexander Graham Bell. They weren't contemporaries." Nina straightened the index finger of the Morse model so it appeared he was about to tap the key to send the first Morse code signal electrically.

"Maybe not," Levi replied. "But I'm working on a theme here. Guess what it is?" He bent the Bell model over so it appeared the wax figure was about to speak into a primitive microphone.

Nina was perturbed. "I'm not Bob, you know. I can see the obvious. The theme is advancement in communications." She raised one eyebrow in a know-it-all look.

"As smart as she is pretty," Levi said without looking up from the Bell model.

Nina blushed.

Levi straightened up. "There." He looked over at Nina, and his smile faltered when he saw her perplexed expression. "What?"

Nina shook her head. "Oh, nothing." She adjusted Bell's right sleeve.

Levi walked over to Nina and leaned against the table next to her. "Nina, I owe you an apology."

"For what?" Nina said with a nervous laugh, pretending to work on rolling up the sleeve.

"For what I said before I left the other night. I have no excuse."

"You were upset."

Levi took hold of Nina's arm and pulled it away from the mannequin. "It was still rude. You were trying to help, and I didn't see it. I try to deal in facts, and when you started talking about monsters jumping out of movies, well, I just couldn't handle it." He looked deep into her eyes. "I'm sorry."

Nina's legs felt weak.

"Whoa there!" Levi held her firmly by the arms and steadied her. "You okay?"

"Didn't eat lunch today," Nina admitted.

"How about I buy us some dinner later, okay?"

"I thought you had that dinner date with Stacy."

Levi grimaced. "I forgot about that."

"That's okay. A promise is a promise. But I'll let you buy me dinner tomorrow night."

"It's a date."

Nina felt her cheeks turn red. But before she could say anything, Levi released her and headed out of the room.

"I left Dad sitting in the Celtic Tribes room," Levi said as he retreated. "He always had a disdain for the Celts."

"Fiends, Ramen noodles, and contour blenders — lend me your steers," Bob was saying at the top of his voice as he placed the victory wreath on a triumphant Julius Caesar.

"Please, Bob," Homer said. "I've had just about enough of this."

"Captain Bob."

"Huh?"

Bob pointed at his hat. "Captain Bob."

"Oh, very well, *Captain Bob*. If you're going to quote Shakespeare, quote him correctly."

"I was in *Julius Caesar*," Bob announced.

"One of the rabble, I presume," Homer said as he moved a small column next to Caesar.

Bob folded his arms and stood next to the conquering general. "Notice the resemblance."

"Someone did a poor job at casting."

"Laugh all you want. I was a great Caesar."

"Promise me that you'll stop misquoting Shakespeare, and I'll let you be the guide in this display."

"Really? Can I wear a toga and a wreath and carry one of those scroll thingies like I saw in a drawing?"

"Yes, just promise."

"Okay," Bob said. "Hey, how long were you with the professor?" Bob asked. No one had seriously mentioned Homer as a possible candidate for Imhotep, but the idea had come to Bob as he worked with the older man.

"Nearly twenty years. He was like a brother to me."

"How come you're not a professor?"

"Never got around to it. I was Professor Tovar's graduate assistant. He took me on all of his digs. I was having such a good time working with the professor and exploring the world that there never seemed to be a good time for it."

"Seems like a waste of time," Bob said, trying to goad the older man.

"That's the difference between youth and maturity." Homer wasn't biting. "I have more knowledge than most of the professors in this field. I learned by hard work, not from some book. Most of the professors in archaeology today think that they can find everything in a computer program or on the Internet. I could run circles around them."

"Yeah. But they have one thing that you don't."

Homer wiped his brow with a handkerchief. "What's that?"

"A piece of paper saying they learned it. What have you got? Wrinkles. You haven't even written a book."

Homer sat up like a defendant on trial. "I assisted Professor Tovar on his books. They're the authority in modern archaeology."

"Your work, his name on the cover."

Homer stood. "Professor Tovar wouldn't have made half of his discoveries without my assistance. We were the best of friends."

"Oh, right. So that's why his son is now in charge of the exhibit, and you're still an assistant."

Homer's face turned red. The tall, thin man straightened to his full height. Bob suddenly had an image of Homer with a fez on his head. Homer pursed his lips, turned, and left the room.

Bob shrugged. He didn't know what information he had gathered, but he had hit a sensitive nerve with Homer.

A scream echoed throughout the building.

Bob snapped out of his reverie. A second scream. Bob dashed from the Roman Empire room. The scream had come from one of the rooms in the future. He darted through the displays and rooms, stopping when he came to the Renaissance room.

At first, he didn't see anything. He scanned the room. On a far wall were some of the more ingenious and terrible torture devices invented in the Middle Ages. Horrors to bring out the truth: the rack, iron boot, iron maiden, vat for boiling, thumb screws —

Bob's eyes went back to the iron maiden. A pair of eyes stared back at him. Large green eyes. Bob ran over to the iron maiden, unlatched the clasp, and opened it.

Stacy fell forward in a swoon. Bob caught her in his arms and gently lowered her to the floor. Fortunately, the iron maiden's deadly spikes had been removed and Stacy was uninjured.

"What are you doing with my prisoner?" came a booming voice.

Bob's head jerked up. A medieval executioner stood over him, ax cradled in his arms.

"Not you again," Bob said with a grimace. "Who turned you on?"

"What are you doing with my prisoner?" the executioner repeated.

Bob tensed. This couldn't be the mechanical

executioner, because it couldn't talk. This executioner was real. Just as quickly Bob's shoulders relaxed.

"You forgot to take off your argyle socks, Marvin," Bob said, pointing to the executioner's feet.

The executioner looked down. "Darn it!" came a whiny voice in place of the deeper one.

"Nice try, though." Bob looked down at Stacy.

Stacy opened one eye. "Is he back?"

"Yes," Bob replied.

Stacy jumped to her feet and punched Marvin. He squealed.

"That's for locking me up in that thing. I almost suffocated."

"You didn't have to punch my nose. I've got sinus problems!"

"You're going to have legal problems when I tell my dad what you did. My dad's a lawyer, and no one messes with a lawyer's daughter."

"Figures," Bob muttered. "Brother, just what we need — a jurist's princess."

Stacy spun on Bob. "Wh —" and then she screamed.

Bob twisted around.

A mummy had silently walked up to the group.

Stacy screamed again and fell to the floor. Marvin followed suit.

"Thanks, guys," Bob said, frowning.

The mummy grabbed Bob by the shoulders and threw him into the iron maiden, slamming the door shut. Through its rectangular peephole, Bob watched as the mummy bent down, picked up Stacy, and disappeared into the labyrinth that was the convention center.

Bob looked down at Marvin.

"Oh, Marvin," Bob called. "Marvin. Marvin!"

But Marvin, the medieval executioner, did not move.

Nina had heard the screams while still in the American Inventors display room. She ran through the labyrinth of human achievement, stopping when she found the executioner lying on the floor of the Renaissance room. She bent down and checked his wrist. Still alive. She pulled off the mask.

"Marvin?" she said.

"Marvin," came a voice behind her.

Nina stood and spun around. She shrieked as a pair of eyes stared out at her from the iron maiden.

"Bob?"

"Bob."

"I ought to slap you. What are you doing in there? You scared me to death."

"Pull up the latch. The mummy's got Stacy."

Nina lifted the latch, and Bob stepped out.

"Imhotep?" Nina said.

"No, one of his minions."

Nina pointed to Marvin. "What's he doing here?"

"He was flirting with Stacy."

Nina raised her hands. "I don't even want to know. Which way did the mummy go?"

"Follow me." Bob waved his hand and trotted into the next room. Nina followed.

"Why does the mummy want Stacy?" Nina said.

"Imhotep has all four of the canopic gods now. It's time to begin the rituals of bringing Anck-Su-Namun back to life."

"How can he do that? He doesn't have the scrolls."

"Maybe he's just getting things ready."

"That means he believes Stacy has the spirit of Anck-Su-Namun in her," Nina said.

"And that he has to kill Stacy to bring his long-lost beloved princess back to life," Bob agreed. They were silent for a minute. "Hey, you know who's missing?"

"Who?"

"Karl Homer."

"Homer?"

"Yeah. I made him mad and he stormed out of here. Then the mummy shows up. Homer didn't come running when Stacy was screaming."

"So, where is he?"

"I'll bet you a ride to school for the rest of the year that he's in the Egyptian room wearing a fez."

"Forget it, Captain Bob. That's a sucker bet."

"I tried."

"Try harder next time."

They entered the Egyptian room and stopped. They scanned the room, but only the two sarcophagi and the relics were in the room.

"No Homer, no Stacy," Bob said.

"This is the way they came, right?"

"It's the only way they could have come. This place goes around like a labyrinth and ends here."

"No, it doesn't," Nina said.

"What?"

"There's one more room: an emergency exit."

"Why didn't you mention this before?"

Nina pointed to the other end of the room. "Because I didn't see *that*." Bob followed her pointing finger until his line of sight rested on the red-letter EXIT sign just above a door.

"Where'd that come from?" he said, knitting his brow.

"It was hidden behind the curtain. The mummy carrying Stacy pushed it aside, but it didn't fall into place. Let's go."

Without hesitation, they both ran to the door and pushed it open.

The room they entered was dimly lit. A lone fluorescent lightbulb cast shadows over the large room.

Bob squinted. "Looks like a storage room."

"Good place to hide a couple of extra mummies. Look." Bob followed Nina's finger until he spied two oblong boxes.

They walked over to the boxes. Bob reached inside, pulling back his hand to reveal a fine gray dust on his skin.

"Mummy dust," he said, wiping his hands on his pants.

They walked among the boxes, stacks of chairs, folded tables, and other accoutrements used by the convention center, but they didn't find the mummy or Stacy.

"The mummy couldn't have backtracked," Nina said. "We'd have run right into it."

"That way, " Bob said, pointing. This time it was Nina's turn to follow Bob's finger, and her eyes fell on another EXIT door.

"This is worse than picking the right door at the fun house," she said.

"But that's the only door to choose. Let's go."

"What are you?" Nina said with a slight smile. "Eddie-Atta-Boy?"

"Just doing my duty." Bob tipped his yacht cap. "I'm off, said the madman."

He hit the door in a full run. It swung open

into the chilly January night. Nina joined him. They looked around quickly.

"There," Bob said, pointing.

A black van sat fifty yards behind the convention center, gray exhaust coming out of the tailpipe into the cold night air. They ran silently to the van and stopped on the driver's side. Bob leaned his ear up against the side of the van.

"Muffled noises," he whispered to Nina.

"Now what? Joe's not here," she whispered back.

Bob pulled away from the van. "What am I? Chopped Spam? We don't always need Joe."

"This is no time to get your ego twisted in a knot."

"I'm not twisting my ego in a knot. I'm saying that we don't have time to go get Joe. Stacy's in here." He jerked a thumb toward the van. "This is the same van Joe described — the one that he was kidnapped in. Stacy's either being prepared to become a mummy or she's having her blood drained out."

"What do you suggest we do? Open the door and yell, 'Surprise!'"

"Something like that."

Nina thought for a moment. "That's not a bad idea."

"You go up front and distract them. I'll pull the back door open, grab Stacy, and then we'll get out of here."

"Okay, but just grab Stacy and get out of there. We don't have time for you to go exploring in there."

"What are you talking about?"

"Never mind. Ready?"

"Ready as I'll ever be."

Nina crouched down and duck-walked to the front of the van. She held up three fingers. Bob nodded. He quickly went around to the back but stayed wide of the rear windows.

"Hey!" he heard Nina yell from up front. Then he heard a pounding on the front windshield. "Hey!" More pounding. "Your mummy wears army boots!"

Corny! Bob thought. *I must be rubbing off on her.* He took a deep breath, grabbed the door latch, and flung the door open.

The mummy was at the front of the van, pounding on the window, trying to get to Nina, who was jumping and shouting. The tall, thin man in the fez sat on the driver's side, holding a plastic blood bag and needle in one hand and a black Egyptian wig in the other. He had been looking at the mummy, but his head spun around when Bob flung open the door. Stacy lay at the bottom of the van, unconscious.

"Ardeth Bey!" Bob exclaimed. He grabbed Stacy's feet. "Not today, you bloodsucker." Bob pulled Stacy by the feet from the van. Then he grabbed her by the shoulders and brought her to a sitting position. As she began to fall forward, Bob knelt down and let her flop across his shoulder. He stood up, turned, and started running for the convention center.

"I got her!" he shouted. "Run, Nina!"

Bob glanced behind him. Nina darted from around the front of the van and started after him. But it was too late. The mummy jumped from the front of the van, grabbed Nina by the shoulder, and threw her to the ground. Bob stopped, turned, and headed back to the van.

"No, Bob!" Nina screamed as she sprang up. She lashed out with her right foot and kicked the mummy in the midsection. The mummy doubled over.

Nina turned and ran to Bob. "Run, you fool, run!"

Bob spun around, adjusted the still-unconscious Stacy on his shoulder, and continued running. As they neared the rear of the convention center, Bob glanced behind him.

"Hey! I thought mummies were supposed to be slow moving and stiff legged," he huffed.

Nina looked behind her. The mummy was gaining on them, pumping his arms and legs like a trained sprinter.

"He must've been stocking up on Gatorade," she said.

"Wh-what's happening?" Stacy said groggily.

"Nothing," Bob said. "Go back to sleep."

Then Stacy screamed.

"My ear!" Bob shouted.

"No! No!" Stacy screamed.

The mummy was an arm's length away from Stacy. He reached out and grabbed her hair. Stacy grabbed his wrist and tried to push the dead pursuer away. "No!" she screamed again.

Nina slapped at the mummy's arm as all three continued toward the back of the convention center. The mummy clawed at Stacy's hair again, and she screamed even louder.

I've had enough of this, Bob said to himself. He shifted Stacy's weight on his shoulder and darted to the left, then to the right. The mummy, his hand entangled in Stacy's hair, whipped one way and then the other. Then it was tumbling, doing jerky somersaults on the ground.

"Smooth moves, Captain Bob," Nina said as she reached the door and flung it open.

Bob bolted inside, with Nina close behind him. She immediately began pushing stacks of chairs in front of the door. Bob deposited Stacy on the ground and went to help Nina. After a few minutes, they stopped, exhausted, their breaths coming in deep, heavy spasms.

"I — don't — hear — anything," Bob gasped.

"Maybe — he — gave — up," Nina added.

The sound of sobbing made them turn their heads. Stacy sat on the ground, her head in her hands. Nina knelt down and put a hand on her shoulder.

"It's all right, Stacy," Nina said in a soft voice.

Stacy sobbed and shook her head.

"Yes, it is. Bob saved you." Nina looked up at Bob. "He's quite the hero when he has to be."

Bob smiled, tipped his hat, and then said, "Any day."

Stacy looked up at both of them. Her cheeks were streaked with tears, her eyes were red, and her mascara made her look like a raccoon.

"My weave!" she sobbed.

"What?" Nina said, confused, looking up at Bob.

"My weave," Stacy repeated, more softly this time.

"Your weave?" Nina said.

"That mummy stole my weave!"

Bob slapped his head. "When he grabbed her hair, he pulled off her weave," he explained, getting it at last. "At least you got out of there with your life."

"Yeah," Stacy said, pulling at her hair. "But now I look stupid."

Bob looked at Nina. "I'll never understand women."

CHAPTER SIXTEEN
Thirty Minutes Later

"Here, try this on." Nina handed a wig to Stacy. The wig had row upon row of black braids, just like the ancient Egyptians wore.

Stacy sneered at the wig. "That doesn't look anything like my weave."

"Just try it on. I want to check something."

Stacy took the wig and put it on, tucking her blond hair up under the wig.

Nina stepped back. "What do you think, guys?"

Joe tilted his head one way and then the other. "I don't know."

"Could be," Bob said.

"A definite maybe," Turner said.

They were sitting in the manager's office of the convention center.

When they didn't hear the mummy outside the door, Bob ventured a peek and saw that the van was gone, as was the mummy. So was Stacy's weave. Then he and Nina coaxed Stacy into going with them to the manager's office, where Nina had called Detective Turner, who had been roused from his lounge chair. Joe had been checking out Karl Homer's record on the Internet.

Marvin had disappeared. Bob searched the center and couldn't find him anywhere. Karl Homer was also missing.

"This is stupid," Stacy said, taking off the wig and throwing it on the desk. "I'm going home. I don't care how much extra credit I need, I'm never coming back to this stupid exhibit." She stood and left the room in a huff, bumping into Levi at the door.

"Hey," he said amiably. "Ready for dinner?"

Stacy squealed and ran from the office.

"What happened?"

"I'll explain later," Nina said. She looked at Bob. "Did she look like Helen Grosvenor to you?"

"Not really," Bob said.

"You think Ardeth Bey is after Stacy?" Turner said.

"Yes," Joe answered. "Ardeth Bey, the man in the fez, sees something in Stacy that reminds him of Anck-Su-Namun."

"And Ardeth Bey didn't look like Homer?" Turner said to Bob.

"No. He looked like the guy in the movie: old and a lot of wrinkles."

"What movie?" Levi said, sitting in the chair Stacy had just vacated.

Bob looked at Joe, who looked at Turner, who looked at Nina. She said, "I told him. He didn't believe me."

"You're still talking about the movie *The Mummy*? Imhotep has stepped off the silver screen and is now stalking Stacy? For what?"

"To bring Anck-Su-Namun back to life," Bob said.

Levi smiled.

"What's so funny?" Bob said through his teeth.

Levi sat up. "Nothing. I'm laughing at myself because I believe you."

"You do?" Nina said, a little enthusiastically.

"Well, I guess I do. I've been around the world and seen some pretty strange things. Some cultures believe that cameras capture the soul and so forbid photography or videotaping anything. Maybe they're right. If they are, then your theory about monsters coming out of their movies makes sense."

Nina was positively beaming.

Bob rolled his eyes. Something about the way Nina looked at Levi bothered him. It was like whenever Nina was around Levi, she wasn't a part of their group any longer.

"We're all ready for the opening on Saturday," Levi was saying. Sweat appeared on his brow. He coughed. "We're going to have a special opening for kids at two P.M., and then the grand reopening and the dedication to my father will be at seven P.M." He coughed again.

Bob had seen this before, a week earlier, when they were all sitting at the Beach Burger.

Levi wiped the sweat from his forehead. "And we're expecting about four hundred people the first night." The last word caught in his throat, and he choked. "Excuse me," he said quickly and left the room. Nina followed.

Bob frowned.

"What's wrong with him?" Turner said.

"He's got claustrophobia," Bob explained. "Bad."

"Do you have a copy of *The Mummy*?" Joe said to Turner.

"You know I do," Turner said. "Why?"

"I want to borrow it and look at it tonight," he explained. "The center will be closed tomorrow, which means that Ardeth Bey will make his move on Saturday, the day of the grand opening. I want to watch the movie and see if I can find any clues." He turned to Bob. "You still have the scrolls hidden?"

Bob nodded.

"Let's go," Turner said, walking out of the room. "I'll give you both a ride home."

Bob walked in silence. Something was gnawing at the back of his brain, like an itch he couldn't scratch. He didn't like the way Levi and Nina were always joking around and hanging around together. Levi was such a know-it-all. Something about Levi. Something about that *name*: Levi.

CHAPTER SEVENTEEN

Saturday
Grand Opening,
Western Civilization Exhibit
San Tomas Inlet Convention Center
7:30 P.M.

"Have you seen Nina?" Bob said hurriedly, trying to keep his feet from getting tangled up in his toga.

"No, I haven't," Hannah replied. "Not since the grand opening."

"Did you see her with Levi?"

"I said I didn't see her, okay?"

"Are you sure?" he asked.

Hannah put her hands on her hips. "I saw your *girlfriend* with Levi, so there." Then she stuck her tongue out at him and stormed away.

"Women," Bob muttered to himself. *What am I saying? Hannah's barely a girl, let alone a woman!*

Bob walked out of the Roman display room and began exploring the other exhibits.

"How goes it?" Joe said. He was wearing the executioner's costume sans ax. "Levi said he thought the ax would look too menacing," Joe explained before Bob could ask.

"You seen Nina?"

"Yeah, she, Stacy, and Levi were back in the Greek exhibit about ten minutes ago. Why?"

"We've got to keep an eye on Stacy, and I don't want Nina running off when we need her."

"I think you don't want Nina hanging around with Levi."

"What do you know about Levi?"

"As much as you do."

"No. I mean about the name *Levi*?"

"Makes a great pair of jeans?"

"I'm serious. Do you know anything about the name?"

"Yeah. It's a Hebrew name. I don't know what it means, though. Why?"

"I don't know yet."

"Sounds like you've got the green-eyed monster on your back." Joe jabbed Bob in the side.

"Where?" Bob looked around.

Joe stopped smiling. "You are serious, aren't you?"

"I'm going to find Nina." Bob walked away from his best friend.

Joe shrugged. He wasn't quite sure what to do, so he decided to keep a distant eye on Bob.

Bob wandered through the exhibits and among the patrons. Some stopped him to ask questions about various displays, but he just mumbled and kept walking. He kept his eye out for any tall, brown-haired girl with a know-it-all look on her face, but he didn't see Nina anywhere. He reached the Egyptian room — still no Nina. He doubled back and made his way slowly through the epochs of time until he reached the twenty-first century. Still no Nina. He blew through his lips. He kept getting tangled in his toga. He had run into Homer a few times and into Detective Turner, who was keeping a sharp eye on Homer, just in case.

Bob started back along the corridors and the displays. His mind raced with the name *Levi*. He felt he had ants in his pants and couldn't get them out. Something about that name. Hebrew. *But what does it mean?*

And where in blazes was Nina?

A familiar giggle broke his trance.

"I'm glad we became friends," Stacy was saying as she and Nina emerged from the women's rest room. "I'm sorry I was so mean in humanities class."

"Let bygones be bygones, I always say," Nina chimed back.

"What does that mean, exactly?"

"Who cares? Pinky shake?"

The two girls shook pinkies and laughed.

"Where have you been?" Bob demanded of Nina.

Nina was in too good a mood. "Been with my new bestest friend." She threw her arm around Stacy.

"Ye-ah, Toga Boy," Stacy said as she tugged on Bob's toga.

"Hey! This might come off and I don't have shorts on!"

"Ooohh!" the girls cried simultaneously.

Then Bob saw what they were wearing. "Why are you two in Egyptian costumes? I thought you guys were in the Middle Ages."

"We were," Stacy said.

"But Levi wants us to help with the Egyptian display the rest of the night and even the rest of the time the exhibit is at the convention center," added Nina

"He says we have real Egyptian queen qualities." Stacy pulled her black braided Egyptian wig on and tucked her blond hair under it.

Bob pulled Nina aside and whispered, "Does she know about . . . you know, the movie and Helen Grosvenor?"

Nina put on her Egyptian wig and began tucking her brown hair under it. "No. I didn't tell her anything. It was hard enough to convince her to come back here to work. She called me last night to thank me for saving her from the guys in the van. We had a good talk and smoothed things over. Besides, look at her. She doesn't look anything like Helen Grosvenor."

Bob took a hard, studious look at Stacy, the Egyptian queen. Nina was right. There was no resemblance.

"Now," Nina continued as she put on the gold headband that secured the wig to her head, "I've turned an enemy into a friend, and we're going to be Egyptian queens for the rest of evening." She gave Bob a gentle shove. "Out of the way, peasant."

The two girls crooked their arms together and disappeared into the crowd headed to the Egyptian room.

Bob didn't know whether to laugh or cry. He had never seen Nina look so — *happy*. He had only met her the previous summer, and then she was always serious, goal-oriented, and didn't have time for trifles or jocularity. Now, she had a boyfriend, a newfound girlfriend, and was laughing all the time. Bob scratched the back of his head.

"Hey, Bob," Joe said, catching up to his friend. "You find Nina?"

"Yeah," Bob said blandly. "She's an Egyptian queen."

"What?" Joe said with a smile.

"She and Stacy are helping in the Egyptian room now. They're dressed up like Egyptian queens. You know, gold headbands and all."

"I'm glad Stacy came back."

"No, wait."

"I'm not glad Stacy came back?"

Bob thought for a moment. "No, I mean, only Nina had a gold headband. Stacy didn't have one. In fact, it wasn't just a gold headband. It was a headband with a cobra sticking up from it."

"A cobra?" Then Joe's eyes widened.

"An Egyptian queen!" Bob cried out. He grabbed Joe by the shoulders. "An Egyptian queen!"

They both turned and bolted through the crowd, bellowing an occasional "excuse me" along the way. When they got to the Egyptian room, the doors were shut.

"Oh, this is just great!" Bob grabbed the door handles and yanked. The doors were securely locked. "Just GREAT!"

Joe pounded on the doors and then tried pushing them open as well. But it was no use.

Bob pulled a the small two-way radio from under his toga. He pressed the speaker button: "Turner, this is Bob. We've got Ardeth Bey in the Egyptian room. He's got Nina."

Bob didn't wait for a reply. He and Joe pounded on the door some more. The visitors nearby began whispering among themselves and started to clear out, not knowing what to think of the two teenage boys in costume banging on the door.

"Ardeth Bey," Bob shouted. "We know you're in there! Open up!"

"You hid the scrolls, right?" Joe said.

"Yeah."

"He can't do anything without the scrolls."

"I know that. Ardeth Bey!" Bob pounded on the door.

"Exactly where did you hide the scrolls?"

Bob stopped pounding on the door. His breathing was deep and choppy. He looked at Joe with blank eyes.

"Where did you hide the scrolls, Bob?" Joe's voice was commanding this time.

Bob pursed his lips and then said hurriedly, "In the legs of the couch."

"The legs of the couch! Why did you hide them there?"

"The last place you expect to find anything is the first place where it was hidden."

"Smooth move, Captain Boob!" Joe's voice was genuinely angry. It was the first time Bob ever remembered Joe being really angry with him.

"Where else was I supposed to hide them?"

A scream came from within the room. Both boys turned and pounded on the door. "Nina! Nina!"

"What's happening?" Turner said as he ran up to the boys.

"What's going on here?" Homer asked as he joined the group.

Turner turned to Homer. "Keep the people out of this area." Homer didn't move. "Now!"

Homer turned and began to gently ask the crowd to move through to the next room, explaining that there were some electrical problems in the Egyptian room. Homer closed the corridor doors, sealing the room off from the rest of the exhibits.

Turner took out his .357. "Stand back." He aimed the gun at the door's top hinge and fired. The gun exploded and the hinge blew apart. He did the same thing to the middle and then the bottom hinges, each with the same result. The door remained standing, however. Joe kicked it and it fell open with a loud thud.

Turner, Joe, and Bob rushed into the Egyptian room. Almost immediately, they were attacked. A giant baboon leaped on Turner, wrested the gun from his grip, and buried its massive teeth into the detective's shoulders. Turner screamed and fell to the floor. He pummeled the baboon, but the monkey held its toothy grip.

The jackal attacked Joe, knocking him to the floor. A sickening wheeze escaped through Joe's lips as he hit the ground. He threw his arms over his face as the jackal leaped on top of him, snapping its massive jaw at his flailing arms.

Bob ducked just as the falcon dove for his head. The enormous bird cried out at the miss, veered up, curved to the left, and began a second dive, talons first, straight for Bob's upturned, face.

Bob fell to the floor and rolled under the table with the queen's artifacts. The falcon slammed into the table, scattering the once-precious items in all directions. The falcon screamed as it hit the wall behind the table.

The mummified cat fell in front of Bob. He picked it up, shot out from under the table, and began thrashing the downed bird with it. The falcon, lying on its back, screamed and tried to grab the cat with its talons, tearing at the ancient wrappings that held it together. Bob used one hand to wallop the falcon over and over again while he grabbed an ornate box with his free hand. He flipped open its lid and slammed the box over the falcon. Then he scooted the box under the table and secured it there.

Bob turned to find Joe beset by the jackal. Bob began hurling stray objects at it, striking the animal about the shoulders and head. The jackal turned, its lips curled back to reveal black gums and fanged teeth. Joe immediately grabbed the jackal by the sides of the neck and began to strangle it. The jackal snapped and snarled, but was helpless. Joe clung to the dog as he made his way to his feet. The jackal snarled again and kicked out with its paws, trying to brace itself against the ground.

"Over here!" Bob shouted. He was holding the exit open. Joe dragged the dog over to the door, threw it inside, and Bob slammed the door shut, locking it.

"Turner!" Joe yelled.

Both boys ran over to Turner, who had managed to get the baboon's teeth out of his shoulder and was now trying to keep the fangs from sinking into his head. Joe grabbed the baboon in a headlock. The primate gasped and clawed at Joe's arms, tearing Joe's shirtsleeves and scratching his skin.

"Choke him until he's blue in the face!" Bob shouted. He walked over to the exit door. "Oh, that's right, baboons are already blue in the face! Ready?" he said to Joe as he unlocked the door again.

"Yeah," Joe said, struggling to hold on to the thrashing baboon. "Now!"

Joe threw the monkey just as Bob flung open the door. The baboon collided with the jackal, who was just about to make a leap for the open door.

"Two with one shot!" Bob yelled, slamming the door shut.

"So much for ancient gods," Joe said with a wry smile.

"Look out," Turner said weakly, then fainted.

Joe turned and then ducked. The Egyptian warrior's silver blade grazed the top of his head. The warrior raised his sword to swing at Bob but stopped midstroke as a deep, guttural voice echoed throughout the room.

The words were foreign and ancient and sounded as though they came from the bowels of the earth.

Bob and Joe faced Ardeth Bey. But this time he wasn't wearing his fez. He had on the ancient robes of a high Egyptian priest, gold embroidered cotton with seams that were so fine they were almost invisible. Over that was a breastplate of gold with the all-seeing eye of Horus engraved upon it. The eye was surrounded by the extended rays of the sun, symbol of Ra, the most high of all Egyptian gods.

And the face that Ardeth Bey wore wasn't the aged, wrinkled face that Bob had seen two days earlier. This face was young, smooth, handsome, full of life — the face of Levi Tovar.

"Levi!" Bob shouted.

The high priest looked at the short freshman.

"Levi," Bob said more softly. "Levi: Hebrew."

He turned to Joe. "Levi is the name of one family of priests in Hebrew culture."

"You will be silent!" The walls of the room shook with the words. Bob and Joe grabbed their throats as some invisible force squeezed their windpipes.

"Stop!" another voice commanded. It came from under the canvas tarp that lay spread over the sarcophagus of the long-dead queen Anck-Su-Namun.

Ardeth Bey, aka Imhotep, pulled the tarp back to reveal the mummified remains of the queen. Beside her lay Nina. She was dressed like an Egyptian queen with a gold cobra crown. The scarab that had adorned the dead queen now rested on Nina's chest. The amulet seemed to glow and pulse with a bluish light. It was as if she was being held down by the force of the light.

Nina looked at her two friends, fear and helplessness in her eyes. "Stop," she said softly, almost crying.

Joe and Bob fell to the floor as the invisible hand ceased choking them. They breathed deeply.

"The scarab," Bob uttered. "It's matching her heartbeat."

"He's got the Scroll of Thoth," Joe said, pointing to the ancient papyrus scripts Imhotep held in both hands.

Imhotep spoke once more in ancient Egyptian, and the warrior came to life. He moved with callous rigidity, marching in straight lines and right angles until he was positioned behind the two teenagers, his sword cocked at their heads.

"If you move, he will cut off your heads," Imhotep said with a thick accent. "You may witness the ceremony of resurrection, but if you interrupt, you will be sacrificed immediately."

Imhotep laid the scrolls next to his ancient dead queen. He bent over her shriveled body, his hand smoothing her brow. "Soon, my love, you'll live again. Soon." He kissed the dried and curled lips.

Bob gagged. Imhotep looked at him and smiled.

"You will experience horrors ten times greater before you die," Imhotep said.

He opened the first scroll and read the incantation of atonement, appealing to the god Ra to show mercy to Anck-Su-Namun, Ra's servant and Imhotep's love.

The room shook with thunder, and lightning flashed from the center of the ceiling, striking the mummified corpse. Nina screamed as the bolt of fiery electricity seared her skin. Tears began to roll down her cheeks.

"You will not cry, my beloved, when you are

joined with your body once again, and we are immortal."

"She's not your queen," Bob blurted.

The warrior cocked his arm back farther.

"You didn't say we couldn't talk," Bob said quickly.

Imhotep smiled and glanced at the warrior. The ancient Egyptian relaxed.

"You will be sacrificed soon enough, and my queen and I will drink your blood to seal our love and our immortality."

"I've got high cholesterol," Bob said.

Joe rolled his eyes.

Imhotep unfurled the second scroll and recited the words written in hieroglyphics. A mist formed in the center of the room. It swirled slowly, growing larger and larger as it floated down toward Nina and the dead queen.

"I'm scared," Nina said, trying to keep her voice from shaking.

"He can't do this," Bob whispered. "We'll think of something."

"What?" Joe said. "We don't even have the camera."

"I don't know. Something."

The mist covered Nina and the queen, shaping itself in their forms perfectly.

Imhotep lifted an urn and began pouring the contents onto the queen. A fine gray powder poured from the urn.

"His dead daddy," Bob commented.

"No," Joe said. "The remains of her stomach, liver, lungs, and intestines."

The dust hit the mist and was transformed into the living organs. They floated above the queen, glistening in the light, and then in the blink of an eye, they spun into the queen's body cavity. Her body swelled and a groan issued from the two blackened and curled lips and rotten teeth. Nina screamed and grabbed her stomach.

"They're her organs," Bob said, terror in his voice. "He's taking her organs."

Imhotep spread out the third scroll and began reading. Nina screamed again as the green-gray mist changed to a bright bloodred.

Bob rolled to one side. The blade of the warrior's sword caught a piece of his toga and sliced it away from his body.

Joe rolled in the opposite direction when he saw his friend take action. The warrior swung at Joe but hit the floor instead.

Bob grabbed what appeared to be an ancient Egyptian broom and swung it at the warrior, striking him in the head. The Egyptian's helmet flew off, revealing a perfectly shaved head. The Egyptian warrior screamed and charged at Bob.

"I think you just made him mad!" Joe yelled.

"Never mind me, get Nina!"

Joe spun around. Nina's face was contorted

in pain. She held her stomach. The mist pulsed with the beat of the scarab. The petrified remains of Princess Anck-Su-Namun twisted and turned and began to suck in the bloodred mist.

"It's sucking the life out of her!" Bob shouted. He ducked as the warrior swung his blade. Bob fell to the floor and crawled under the table. He grabbed the box with the falcon inside it. When the Egyptian warrior bent over to spy his quarry, Bob jerked open the lid of the box and thrust the angry falcon toward him.

The warrior screamed as the falcon sunk its talons deep into the flesh of his face. Blood spurted from the wounds, and the falcon, maddened to the point of dementia, clawed the skin from the Egyptian's face. He dropped his sword, staggering back, trying to pull the bird from his face.

Bob grabbed the sword, and with one swing chopped the falcon in half and cut the head off the Egyptian. The two dead demigods fell to the floor, where they instantly decomposed into fine gray ash.

Joe struggled to pull Nina from the table, but the mist held her like a vise. He felt his own skin and blood being drawn from him wherever the bloodred mist touched him, the pain so intense that he screamed.

Nina was unconscious — or dead. Bob couldn't tell which.

Imhotep had the final Scroll of Thoth, the scroll that would complete the transference of Nina's soul, her essence, into Anck-Su-Namun. Already, the queen was taking on the shape of her once-great beauty, and Nina was withering before their eyes.

Imhotep spoke the final words in his thick accent: *"Oh! Amon-Ra — Oh! God of gods — Death is but the doorway to a new life — We live today — We shall live again — In many forms shall we return — Oh, Mighty One."*

The walls exploded with the sound of thunder. Nina screamed; the sound was the most heart-wrenching Bob had ever heard. Every atom in his body shook from the vibration of Nina's scream. Joe, too, was beginning to shrivel as the bloodred mist started to absorb his life force. Imhotep's eyes glowed with a sickening yellow gleam.

"No!" Bob yelled. He ran to Nina and grabbed the scarab from atop her chest.

Instantly, the mist dissipated. The screaming stopped but was replaced by a moan of such despair that Bob thought he could hear the hounds of the underworld baying in response.

The gleam in Imhotep's eyes faded. A look of horror crossed his face.

"This is it, isn't?" Bob yelled above the roar and the moans of death. "This is it. This is how I'm going to send you back — send you to hell!"

Imhotep moved around the table toward Bob. Bob backed up, holding the scarab in front of him.

"You want this? You want this?"

A growl issued from the lips of the priest. "You will return the scarab before it's too late, before the process reverses itself."

Bob threw the ancient scarab onto the floor and then stepped on it, pulverizing the amulet into dust.

Imhotep screamed as he looked down at the destroyed scarab. He knelt down and ran his fingers through the dust as though he could somehow put the thing back together.

Bob ran over to the table. Joe was kneeling beside the table, one arm still over Nina as if he were trying to still pull her from the table. Nina lay still and quiet. Bob watched in fascination as the color returned to her skin and the skin began to smooth out and lose its deep wrinkles.

It was some moments before they realized that the dead queen was no longer lying beside Nina. He spun around. Kneeling next to Imhotep was the half-resurrected Princess Anck-Su-Namun. Bob grimaced at the sight: parts of Anck-Su-Namun's body were whole, while other parts of her body had yet to rejuvenate, exposing muscle, tissue, sinew, veins, and bone.

Imhotep wept. Anck-Su-Namun put a bony arm around her love. He turned to her. Only half her face had been completed. One half was beautiful, with full red lips, a high cheekbone, smooth dark skin, and a large round eye surrounded by heavy black makeup; the other half was skull and tissue. She leaned over and placed her half lips on Imhotep's lips. They kissed long and deep.

Pity rose within Bob, and he choked. Then the bodies of Imhotep and his beloved Anck-Su-Namun crumbled into dust.

EPILOGUE

Sunday

11:30 P.M.

Captain Bob's Room

Captain Bob placed his fingers on the keyboard as though he were greeting a long-lost friend. His report card had arrived on Saturday: B's and C's, up from the D's and F's he'd gotten last term. His mother had given him permission to use his computer again and it felt like Christmas, his birthday, and the Fourth of July all at the same time.

He clicked the "connect" button, and the computer jumped to life. The home page of his favorite website flashed on the screen. He typed in his user name and password and began recounting the sad story of their battle with the Mummy for all of his faithful readers, just as he had done for Dracula, the Wolf Man, and Frankenstein. He ended the story by saying that he felt sorry for Imhotep. All he wanted was to be reunited with his long-lost love. He was lonely.

"We all get lonely sometimes," Bob wrote. "I think I know why Nina wanted someone to be with so badly.

"We found Stacy stuffed in Imhotep's coffin. She wasn't as upset about being put in a coffin as you'd think she'd be. She's really changed from being a total snot to actually being kind of cool. She said it was better than having Imhotep trying to kill *her*.

"Detective Turner lost a lot of blood, but he's going to make a full recovery. He was told by the chief of police to stay away from any more cases that we're involved in, since this is the second time in two months that he's been laid up.

"Nina is okay, too. She still has the stomach cramps, but she's back to her old self. Well, almost. She seems a little sad. Joe says that it's because she has matured. I told Joe that he was full of it. Nina's just recovering from the shock of sharing her guts with a dead mummy queen. She'll get over Levi. Joe said that Levi was the first boy she had ever been serious about. If that's true, she picked the wrong guy to fall for. And, man, did she fall!

"Joe still thinks I was jealous of Levi. I told him what he could do with himself.

"The best Joe and I can figure out is that the Scroll of Thoth and the scarab acted as a conduit for Imhotep and his horde to be placed back into *The Mummy*. We didn't have the camera with us this time. In fact, Nina insists it still wouldn't have worked, just like in *Frankenstein*. When we got to Joe's house late last night, Joe put the special 3-D DVD disk into his player, and, sure enough, there was Imhotep, aka Ardeth Bey, in all his glory. We should have caught on about Levi much earlier — I mean, what mummy wouldn't be claustrophobic after centuries of being cooped up in a tomb?

"The exhibit is still open if any of you want to come visit it. Joe and I quit once we caught the Mummy, but you'll find Nina there most nights. She just kind of wanders around looking sad and lonely. Stacy's there, too. So far, Stacy and Nina are still friends. That's good because Nina needs all the good friends she can get right now.

"We've got spring break coming up week after next. But it won't be much of a spring break for Nina, Joe, and me. I got a call this afternoon from my friend Skylar Crockett, who lives near the NASA Causeway. He's the one who called a few weeks ago and told me about the half-eaten dolphins and sharks and about the fishermen who were attacked by a giant manlike fish. Skylar says he saw this manfish creature. He's a classic horror nut like the rest of us, so I guess he knows a Gill Man when he sees one.

We'll be going down there next Saturday — what a way to spend spring break!

"I've got to sign off for now. I've got a vocab test in Ms. Bashara's class, and the new biology teacher, the one who replaced Dr. James, wants me to help with a lab. I said okay, but don't turn into a mad scientist. She just looked at me like I'm crazy.

"I'm off, said the mad man."

Captain Bob

About the Author

Since childhood, Larry Mike Garmon has been an aficionado of things that go bump in the night. Watching such classic horror movies as *Frankenstein* and *Psycho* added to his anxiety about strangers with glowing eyes. Reading horror comic books and tales of terror from Edgar Allan Poe, Nathaniel Hawthorne, H. P. Lovecraft, and Ambrose Bierce compounded his concern, but also encouraged him to try writing scary stories of his own. He often listens to Bach and Metallica while writing his creepiest scenes.

Larry Mike lives with his wife, Nadezhda, in Altus, Oklahoma. They have five children — three grown and two still in school. Larry Mike is an English teacher at Altus High School, while Nadezhda is a pianist and vocalist. They have two dogs, two cats, and a vintage 1965 Buick Wildcat.

Although Larry Mike still enjoys a good horror movie or novel, he says there is nothing more horrifying than teaching a room full of teenagers! He is an active member of the Horror Writers Association, and can be reached at MonsterMan@LarryMike.com.